THE MAGE VAMPIRE HYBRID

The Paranormals of Ahl Book 2.5

ML CONKLIN

Thank you for choosing this book. I cannot begin to express how grateful I am, and I hope you enjoy it.

The Mage Vampire Hybrid is a shorter book from the POV of a side character in the Paranormals of Ahl series. It explains how Lily, the hybrid found at the end of Bug Magic, landed on Quin's doorstep. If you haven't read The Dragon Problem (Book 1) and Bug Magic (Book 2), I suggest you start there, or some things might not make sense.

Trigger warnings and heads-up:

1. A reference to past child abuse, including attempted SA (no details).

2. Violence and gore throughout the book.

3. A cussing gnome and other profanity.

4. A no spice budding romance (does not fully develop in this book).

5. The romance has an age gap (I know some people don't like that).

CHAPTER ONE

ADRENALINE SPIKED AS I crouched on the roof, making it hard to keep my fangs from popping out. I blended into the shadows and swiped a stray curl out of my face. My prey hopped the curb and stuffed his hands in his jacket pockets as he shuffled down the sidewalk. I summoned more shadows. With only one chance to get it right, I needed to be smart and fast. Coiled, ready to strike, I waited. Three more steps. Two. One.

"I know you're there, Lily, so you might as well give up."

"Dang it, Alex!" I let the shadows go and hopped off the roof in one fluid motion. I landed in a crouch in front of my brother and retracted my fangs. "What gave me away?"

He pushed his unneeded glasses up his nose. "I dunno. Your scent, your sound, that you suck at blending into the shadows. Oh, and I read your mind."

"I'm not that bad at blending in." Alex's mental magic, mixed with his shifter senses, made him hard to surprise. I hadn't been able to sneak up on him in years. It made me feel inept. "You're just... Well, you."

He shook his head as he opened the door and waved me ahead of him. "No. You're just bad at being a vampire."

I scurried through the door. "Whatever. I'll get you one day, and you'll never see it coming."

"That's debatable."

The smell of stale alcohol and fried food made my nose crinkle. "Busy for a Tuesday night."

The bar, Hooves, was in a hybrid neighborhood in west Boise and owned by a satyr-centaur. He designed it after a pub his mom owned in Ireland, but with an American twist. Deep wood bar stools lined a long bar, taking up most of the main area. Each end had three dark green booths, with a smattering of two-person, dark wood tables and chairs along the front.

I spotted the owner, Dale, behind the bar. In his human form, he resembled a big teddy bear with his wide shoulders and scruffy brown hair and beard. His surly expression ruined the image as he mixed a drink and slammed it down in front of a patron.

We took two empty stools at the far end by the wall. I wanted a drink more than a fight, and Dale had a nasty temper and a butt-load of magic. I folded my hands and scanned the crowd while we waited for him to notice us.

Most of the customers were other hybrids with different magical backgrounds. Two humans sat at the center of the bar, slumped over their bottled beer. Regulars who lived near the hybrid subdivision. My eyes stopped on a table on the far side where four purebloods sat, sipping their beers. They watched the hybrids with an intensity that made my skin crawl. It wasn't unusual for purebloods to be scattered throughout the hybrid community. But the ones I knew were usually part of a mixed magic couple or lone shifters. It was unusual for two mid-level mages and two witches to hang out anywhere in Boise. Especially since Allure, one of the biggest pockets in the world, was nearby.

I leaned closer to Alex. "Can you get a read on those guys?"

"Too much noise to open the channel."

"Are they the ones following you?"

For the last month or so, Alex was being followed. It kicked my protective instincts into high gear and made me paranoid, even though he wasn't worried about it. They were weak in magic, and he was confident he'd win if they tried to attack him.

Two craft beers landed in front of us, followed by two meaty hands.

I guessed we were drinking beer. "How's it hangin', Dale?"

"Long and thick, with a curve to the right," the barkeep answered without missing a beat. "Got a new local supplier and need an honest opinion. They're on the house." He knocked twice on the bar and went back to work.

I wasn't a fan of beer, so I tried not to let my face pucker with the first sip.

Alex set his phone down. "Dale must be hard-up for an opinion if he asked you to sample beer."

"Looks like it." I schooled my face and took another sip. The bitterness wouldn't disappear until I had a few drinks. I took a third gulp, shook my head, and set the glass down. At least it gave me a focus. I closed all my senses except my hearing.

Scents and sight melted away as I focused on sound. My ears were far more sensitive than humans, even without a focus. But once focused, it was almost as good as a shifter's. Except they couldn't target specific conversations.

I listened to two hybrid women on our side of the room. They were worried about their gardens. I tuned them out and moved on. A young couple discussed their sex life. Not going there. I was suffering a dry spell and practiced the out-of-sight, out-of-mind theory, so it didn't interest me. I skipped them and focused on the purebloods.

"What do you suppose he is?"

"Nothing exciting."

"We're here for the guy at the end of the bar?"

My ears perked up at their mention of Alex.

"The one next to the vampire?"

"Yes."

"Shifter."

"Not only a shifter. Also, a strong mental mage. That's why the boss wants him."

"What's so special about a filthy hybrid?"

"Not our problem. We have our orders."

With a sharp inhale, I ripped my focus away. "They said their boss wants you for your mental magic."

Alex put a hand on my arm. "It doesn't matter, so stop worrying. We'd take them out without breaking a sweat."

I'd been over-protective of my little brother since my parents brought him home when he was seven. The kid was so small and so beat up that my heart broke for him, and I swore I'd protect him with my life. I still felt that way, but if I were to be honest with myself, he didn't need my protection anymore. He had unique mental mage skills and could shift into a giant cat. On top of that, the same powerful parents trained us.

My instincts didn't care. "If they do anything, it's going to get ugly. And you know purebloods are like cockroaches. Where there's one, there's a hundred. If they show up in numbers, we're screwed."

"I'm going to tell Mom and Dad that you called them cockroaches."

"Real mature." I elbowed him for good measure. Our parents were more than just your regular pureblood. Dad was an ancient and powerful being who came from a different realm and created shifters. And Mom was the only sorceress in the world. She could combine witch and mage magic to create a unique blend of spells that no one except maybe the Queen of Ahl herself could break. "They're going to be trouble. I can feel it."

"We'd wipe the floor with those shitheads. Though you might need to use your magic. Then we'd have to avoid the bar for a couple of weeks so the crazies can't swarm you." The little shit snickered.

He was right, though. The hybrids in the bar wouldn't hesitate to kick them out on their butts if they tried anything. Dale alone was enough of a deterrent, so I doubted they'd cause problems. Besides, I hated using my magic. It was dark and attracted every mentally unstable or fanatical human for miles. "Fine."

By the time I finished the first beer, I couldn't taste the bitterness, so I didn't hesitate to sip the second one. It had a floral undertone that would probably stick on the roof of my mouth for days.

Alex motioned with his hands as he explained a new online game he found. I listened but kept my eye on the purebloods. When the four guys settled their tab and left, I stared them down until the door closed behind them, then turned my full attention to my brother.

He loved gaming because he could talk to people online without hearing their thoughts. During face-to-face conversations, he often caught things he had no business hearing. The games helped him socialize. The only person he could stand for long periods of time was me because my vampire nature made me hard to read. He still could if he tried, but didn't bother most of the time.

I finished the second beer and slid the glass forward when a prickling stabbed through my chest. I tried to stay casual. A vampire was close. And I only got the prickly feeling with blood relations. I scanned the bar to find the culprit. A petite brunette sat at the end on the other side of a regular.

I hadn't seen her before she appeared on the stool, which meant she was old. I focused on Dale until I caught his eye, then flipped my eyes to her.

He gave me a slight nod before saying something to the regular. I watched as the guy stumbled off his bar stool and out the door.

I settled my gaze back on the vampire. The tightness in my shoulders eased when her head turned toward me, and I saw she wasn't feral. Feral or angry vampires had a red tinge to their eyes. Hers were brown.

A small smile touched her lips.

The prickling in my chest increased. "Aw, hell."

Alex set his beer on the coaster. "Feral?"

"Worse. Blood relation." I'd noticed more vampires in the city lately, so I'd steered clear. I couldn't have them reporting my presence. But I knew eventually they'd sense me and come closer. Once they caught my scent, they were like bloodhounds. What I didn't account for was a blood relation showing up.

I was still trying to decide what to do when the vampire winked and slunk out the door.

Dale sauntered over and cleared our beers. "You need to leave, Lily. She's not the only pureblood vampire in the area."

My eyes narrowed. "I noticed. What do you know about it?"

He shook his head. "Only that they're following those other purebloods around." He pointed toward the door. "That one hovered outside until well after closing last night."

"Is there a problem in Allure?" Allure was a hidden pocket, or mini realm, where most purebloods lived. There were several of them around the world. Humans couldn't access the pockets, and hybrids weren't welcome, so we lived in the surrounding areas and only went inside when we had to.

He shrugged. "Isn't there always?"

Alex slid off his barstool. "Dale's right. We can't stay here with the purebloods hanging around."

"Fine." I slid off the barstool and walked Alex to his car. I was extra vigilant, but tried not to let my nerves show. If the purebloods were flooding the area, it would screw up my life. I'd worked hard to stay hidden since I escaped Allure as a kid. With the help of our parents, I'd succeeded. If that pureblood reported my whereabouts to the wrong person, I'd be screwed.

Alex closed his eyes when we got to his car. "I'm not getting any thoughts. They're gone."

"Good. Go home and stay behind the wards. I'll meet you there."

I went fluid and stopped in the shadows on the edge of the parking lot to watch over him. My movement so fast that human eyes wouldn't register me. One of my favorite tricks was to zip by people and make them think they saw a ghost, especially around Halloween, which was coming up in a couple of months. I needed to start plotting my route soon.

My brother pulled out of the parking lot and disappeared around the corner. As I turned and headed down the empty street, a tingle between my shoulder blades made me pause. I was being watched. With a curse, I picked up the pace and scanned the street like a human woman would if she walked in the dark alone. I didn't see anyone. Still, that tingle didn't go away.

My biological father found me a couple of months earlier. As a prince of vampires, he thought it was beneath him to speak to his abomination of a daughter, so he sent his minions. When that didn't work, he sent spies. Every time I beat one within an inch of their life, he'd send another like his house members were replaceable. The asshole.

As I rounded the corner, I blended into the shadows of someone's hedges. It didn't take long for a silhouette to appear. Spy number three, for sure.

My heart pounded in my chest as he rounded the corner.

The presence drew closer.

I crouched.

He stopped and swung his head from side to side.

Not yet.

The guy shuffled past my hiding spot.

I pounced.

My fangs popped out, and claws sprung from my hands. I landed on the guy, giving him three quick punches in the stomach using my claws, and kicked the side of his knee. I was so fast he didn't know I was there until he crumpled to the ground. My claws retracted, and I gave him a few regular punches to the face.

If I went much further, I'd call attention to myself, so I disengaged and stepped back. "Who sent you?"

He surged to his feet. The wounds on his face melted away, which meant he was an older vampire. Young vampires took longer to heal. Except me, who healed every bit as fast as him. But then, I was the exception to a lot of rules.

He brushed off his pristine suit. "Your father wishes to meet with you."

"No."

He raised an eyebrow. "You cannot deny Master Jedediah."

I slammed my hands on my hips. "Who's going to stop me? You?" Because of my mixed heritage, I was much more powerful than most vampires. I doubted even good ole Jed could take me down.

"Master Jedediah insists you return to his house."

I went fluid, punched him in the face, and returned to my spot before his head snapped back. "I'll make you a deal. You leave me alone, and I'll stop kicking your ass."

"I cannot." He held out a business card. "You need to contact your father as soon as possible. It is of the utmost importance. He ordered me to inform you he wishes to reconnect."

My biological father had the emotional IQ of a turnip. He didn't love anyone but himself. I'd learned that firsthand when he tried to kill his twelve-year-old daughter. "That's the best joke I've heard in a long time. Hilarious." I didn't laugh. "And a crock of shit. He wants something from me. And honestly, I don't give a damn what it is."

The guy thrust the card toward me. "Please take this, Mistress."

I snatched it out of his hand and went fluid, only stopping when I got to the corner near where I left my van. I never parked at the bar because there was only one exit. That way, we could escape if Alex's car got trapped in the parking lot. In a community of supernaturals pretending to be human, it wasn't uncommon for trouble to start at the hybrid bar. Having a car stashed a few streets away had saved us more than once.

I pulled the shadows around me and sent my senses out. It unnerved me how easy it was for Jedediah to find me. Between him and the purebloods flooding the city, dodging them was becoming a common occurrence. I shook my head. They weren't my problem. Well, Jed was. But I'd tell my adoptive parents about the encounter, and they'd take care of him. Then, I could go back to looking for strays to save and focus on my deliciously toxic workplace.

When I didn't sense anyone other than the regular hybrids that lived in the neighborhood, I trotted around my minivan. And stopped in my tracks.

Leaning against the driver's side was the most beautiful creature I'd ever seen. And I hadn't sensed him.

The mountain of a man shifted, causing his massive muscles to ripple.

I jerked my eyes to his face, but that wasn't much better. The guy was handsome. He had a square jaw and amazing cheekbones. His long, dark blonde hair cascaded over his wide shoulders in waves. The tan that peeked through his clothes looked airbrushed on by an artist. The most amazing electric-blue eyes I'd ever seen stared back at me, an inquisitive look in them. Power and masculinity radiated off him in waves.

I licked my lips. "Well, aren't you a tall drink of water?"

The man's too-perfect eyebrows drew together. "I am a god, not a beverage."

"The god of thunder?"

"Manipulating elements is not part of my skill set."

My eyes swept over him again. He wore a cotton tunic the color of mud. His pants were too tight and made from some kind of canvas. The knee-high boots were soft leather. All the flirtatious fun drained out of me. I didn't believe he was a god, though.

I shook my head. It wasn't my job to judge. My job was to rescue strays. "Where'd you get those clothes?"

"From home. I was told they would help me blend into this realm."

I wasn't sure if I believed him. It was nearly impossible to jump realms. "Those clothes worked a few centuries ago, but not now. How long have you been here?"

"I arrived today." He pointed toward the bar. "That vampire you fought was the first supernatural I encountered, so I followed him. Why did you let him live?"

"None of your business."

"He will report your behavior to his housemaster, as well as yours."

"Not my problem. And I don't have a housemaster, nor do I want one." I held up a hand. "And how do you know about housemasters if you just got to this realm?"

His perfect brow furrowed. "I studied before my arrival."

My eyes swept over him again. "Not very well."

"What does that mean?"

"If you studied so much, then you'd know to wear jeans and T-shirts." I motioned toward my own clothes. "Or have you not seen a single person yet?"

With a flash of light, his outdated clothes turned to jeans and a black T-shirt that stretched over his muscles and made those electric blue eyes stand out more. "Is this proper?"

I fought the urge to gape. Or drool. The guy was hot. "I suppose. What do you plan to do here?"

"I would like to establish myself and gain followers. Though, I don't know where to start. I hoped to gain information from that vampire's house, but you are far more interesting."

"No, I'm not." I motioned toward my van. "You're blocking the door."

"Yes."

An awkward silence followed. When my patience wore thin, I crossed my arms. "I need you to unblock it so I can leave."

He extended a hand, and I jumped back. My fangs popped out on reflex. How embarrassing. I snapped them back in. "Whoa, big guy. No touching."

He dropped his hand. "My apologies. I thought people in this realm clasped hands when meeting someone new."

"Shake hands, yeah. That's a human thing." Either this guy really was new to the realm, or he was a fantastic actor. My shoulders slumped. He needed help, and I was obligated to find and help strays. It's what my family did. We found strays and misfits and helped them assimilate into the hybrid community. Everything else, like working in the toxic human workplace and beating up Jed's goons, was just entertainment. I pondered whether the so-called god qualified as a rescue. "Why establish yourself in this realm?"

A satisfied smile ghosted across his face. "I am the God Cavilourianabalvivelario. I wish to establish myself *and* find enough worshippers to sustain my power level."

It wasn't my business what he did once he got on his feet, but that sounded extreme. "And you don't know where to start?"

"Correct."

I shook my head and hoped I didn't regret my decision. "Cav—say your name again."

"Cavilourianabalvivelario."

I still didn't get it. "Right. Do you have a place to stay while you set up your cult?"

His gaze drifted into the distance. "There are many things about this world that I do not understand, even with a copious amount of studying."

"I'll take that as a no." I swept my eyes over his amazing body again because I could. "I'm Lily. My family helps lost people establish themselves. If you want, we can get you some more modern clothes, something to eat, and a temporary place to stay."

He straightened. "You would do that for me?"

"Well, yes. Sort of. I'll get you settled tonight, and my parents will decide whether they want to keep helping you tomorrow. If so, they might introduce you to some other purebloods, if that's what you want."

His smile was so potent I had to lock my knees to keep from stepping back and shielding my eyes. "I accept your hospitality."

I ignored the heat that spread through my body. "Right. Get in the van, and I'll get you settled."

CHAPTER TWO

THE GUY DIDN'T KNOW how to open the door and buckle his seatbelt. I walked him through it and sent the standard group text to my family that we used when we found a lost person.

Found a stray. Going to Maria's

Mom:

Alerting Maria

Dad:

The only safehouse available is the farm. It's fully stocked.

Alex:

Backup?

Maria's, the farm, no backup. Thx.

I probably should have taken Alex's offer of backup, but he needed to get his ass home and behind the wards, especially with a bunch of purebloods following him around.

I put my phone away and noticed the guy—I refused to call him a god—staring at it. "Okay, here's how this works. I'll take you to our intake center. My friend Maria will supply you with enough stuff to get started."

"Stuff?"

"Clothing, hygiene items, electronics, and other necessities."

He pointed at my phone. "Will I get one of those?"

"Sure. We'll get a laptop, too, so you have a bigger screen to plan your world domination. First things first, we need to change or alter your name." I jerked a thumb toward myself. "For example, my given name is Liliana. I use the same surname as my adopted parents, First, so my full name is Liliana First, but people call me Lily. It's easier to say and remember. We need to do the same for you, so you fit in better."

"I like Liliana."

"Not if you value your life, you don't." I took a deep breath. "I hate the name, so please call me Lily."

"You are formidable, so I shall call you Lily."

"Whatever. Let's figure out a more earth-friendly one for you."

"You will help me pick one?"

"Yes. Say it again, but as slow as possible."

"Ca-vil-our-ian-abal-viv-el-ar-io."

I tapped the steering wheel with my fingers. "Say the last part again, starting with the 'V' sound."

"Vivelario."

"I suggest you go by the first name, 'Cavil,' and the surname of either Vivelario or Velario. You don't have to use either of those if you don't like them," I added when he didn't comment.

The deep, warm sound of his laughter sent shivers through my body. "I shall henceforth be known as the God Cavil Velario, a name bestowed upon me by the Lady Lily First."

I cleared my throat. "Yeah. Leave out the god part. And the part about me giving you the name, especially the title of lady. It soooo doesn't fit. Just introduce yourself as plain old 'Cavil Velario.' It'll add to your mystery and intrigue." It would also confuse a lot of high-powered paranormals who could read magic. Too bad I wouldn't be around to see the look on their faces.

Thanks to my mage heritage, I could read magic types and levels. The guy's magic was unlike anything I'd ever felt. The stuff was clean and bright. It reminded me of the sunshine peeking out after a heavy rain. I inhaled to tamp down the quiver that ran through my body. His scent matched his magic. I needed to get him to the safe house and be done with the guy.

We pulled into the warehouse parking lot we used to supply hybrids fleeing the supernatural pockets because of harassment and death threats. Most were kids whose parents abandoned them outside the pocket's gates to avoid embarrassment. Assholes. Others were mixed magic couples who refused to hide their bond. My parents established an entire network who looked for them, took them in, and taught them how to live in the human world. It helped, but it wasn't ideal, according to my mom.

Maria, the woman who ran the supply network, had a special type of magic that allowed her to fulfill needs. Several wealthy supernaturals funded her operation and allowed her to operate without considering the cost of supplying the strays we found.

The side door of the massive warehouse swung open as we got out of the car. She wrapped me in a hug before I could dodge. I blamed it on the hunky god stealing my attention. Maria turned to said hunky god and swept her eyes over him. "And who do we have here?"

He stepped forward and stretched out his hand. "I am Cavil Velario. I recently moved to this realm and plan to gain status and worshippers."

Unlike me, Maria had no problem shaking his hand. "I'm Maria. Come inside. Do you have a place for him, Lily?"

"Yeah. Dad's giving him the farmhouse."

"Perfect. Order him some food." She patted his arm. "The poor thing's starving, but too proud to say so. Barbeque, if you can get it."

I took out my phone and flipped open the app. It was getting late, and most places were closed, but I found one and ordered a feast. "Anything to drink?"

"Soda will do nicely."

She dragged Cavil toward the back of the warehouse as I waited out front. I texted the family, letting them know everything was fine. Then made a mental note to warn them about his weirdness before they descended on him in the morning. That could wait until I got him settled.

An hour later, I loaded an enormous amount of clothes, toiletries, and electronics into the back of my van. Cavil picked up a box and fought to figure out how to open the sliding back door.

I tried not to notice how the new navy-blue polo shirt and jeans enhanced his perfect body. "Push the button on the handle."

His eyebrows drew together as the door slid open.

I choked back a laugh. "It's electronic and runs off a battery."

"I see." He shoved the box inside and eyed the door.

"Get in. I'll close it.

When I climbed into the driver's side, a radiant smile lit up his face. "You have truly saved my life, Lily. I will fit in now."

Yeah, not likely. The guy would stand out like a sore thumb based on hotness alone.

He asked me a million questions about using his new phone as we drove. So many that I had a headache when we pulled into the gravel driveway that led to the small two-story farmhouse. Trees and a white fence surrounded the house, giving it privacy from the farmer who leased the adjacent field and the main road.

The only neighbor was half-a-mile west. That property was owned by yours truly. My parents bought the farmhouse when the farmer who previously owned it put it up for sale because he thought the neighbors were evil.

That guy was awful. He'd sit in the side yard and take pot-shots at us whenever we entered the field between our houses. We built a maze in it to mess with him and give us some concealment.

He called the police. When he couldn't get the cops to believe him, the farmer bought a sniper rifle with a scope. I had to use vampire persuasion to make him stop shooting. Bullets hurt. That's when I learned how awful I sucked at vampire persuasion. It wore off, and he claimed we were evil government plants trying to mind-control him and put the farm up for sale.

My parents snatched the property up to prevent me from, and I quote, 'harassing innocent humans.' Cavil was the first to occupy the place since they'd bought it.

I made Cavil unlock the door, so he knew how to get in, and we hauled the massive number of items inside.

"I do not understand why there's so much."

"Maria likes to make sure people don't need to jump into the community until they're ready. You have more to learn than most." I added another box to his load. The fewer trips, the better.

"I am a god."

"So I've heard."

He put two massive boxes down on the tiled entryway. "I have superior blessings, including the ability to learn fast. With your generous help, I will assimilate without delay."

"Sure." I rummaged through the pile of stuff, pulled the laptop out, and shoved it into his hands. Maria set it up to access both the internet and the maginet. "Let's get started."

We set up at the kitchen table, and I scooted two chairs together. It turns out he wasn't lying when he said he was a fast learner. His brain processed information as fast as the computer, and he didn't forget anything. It made me feel inferior and impressed me at the same time. Thanks to my vampire side, I had an excellent memory, but it paled in comparison to his.

I left him to it and hauled his stuff to the master bedroom and put it away. After making the bed, I left Maria's instruction sheet and personal hygiene items on the bathroom counter.

When I returned, Cavil stared into space as he rubbed his chin.

"You okay there, big guy?"

"The supernatural culture differs from the human culture. Do you know why?"

"Probably because of the separation. Most purebloods stay in their pockets and only use the human world as a playground. They like to steal human inventions and use them to create their magical versions. You'll find the hybrid community has a mixture of both cultures. We operate under human laws, and some have adopted human values."

"I do not understand the references. What is the difference between purebloods and hybrids?"

The explanation was going to take a while, so I plopped into a chair. "Not much, really. Purebloods only have one type of magic. Like a mage, a vampire, or a shifter. Hybrids result from two or more magic types having children. Magic doesn't transfer like DNA." I held up a hand. "Do you know what that is?"

He tapped on his laptop and read. After a couple of minutes, he nodded. "I will study it more, but I understand the reference."

"I'm no expert on DNA, but magic doesn't work the same way. It's more generous and pickier. When two different magic types have a kid, magic chooses what powers to give them. Most of the time, the kid inherits both. If two hybrids have kids, each one will inherit two of the four magic types. Are you following so far?"

"Yes."

"My adoptive parents are purebloods. My dad is the first shifter to exist in this realm. He created the shifters, and the purebloods refer to him as a First. My mother is the last sorceress. They had three biological kids over many years. All three inherited both magics. It gave them rare but similar abilities. Hybrids are usually pretty badass because we get a full dose of both magics. Then it integrates, so we're kind of like our own magical type. It makes us twice as powerful as your average pureblood."

"Us?"

"Yeah. My brother is an American Lion-Mage hybrid. He has unique mental magic and can use it in animal form and do a partial shift. All because the two magics mixed. He doesn't have two magics, but one that incorporates both. Does that make sense?"

"Somewhat."

"Okay." I drummed my fingers on the table. "How about this? He's larger than the average lion shifter and more powerful than other mental mages because he has a double dose of magic. Since they mixed, he can use them at the same time." I jerked a thumb toward myself. "I'm a natural-born vampire-mage with both magical powers. My vampire powers are hundreds of years ahead of made vampires my age. I don't use my mage powers often because they're dark. But I can use both at the same time."

Cavil leaned forward. "Except you are neither of those."

"Huh? Uh. Yes, I am. My biological mother is a powerful mage, and my biological father is a vampire. So that's exactly what I am."

He shook his head. "I will need to learn more about the realm before I can explain it. I am a god, Lily, which means I can read powers. You are neither a mage nor a vampire."

"Yeah, because I'm both." I flipped my fangs out and opened my mouth. "Thee. Thangs."

"You only prove my point. My studies indicate vampires have two fangs, not four."

"Natural-born vampires have four." I waved a hand. "Look, I know who my parents are. Trust me when I say I'm a mage-vampire hybrid."

"Perhaps."

There was no getting through to the guy, so I retracted my fangs and snatched the phone out of his hand. "Once you learn more about this realm, you'll see what I mean. Now, let me program your phone so you can get ahold of me and my parents if you need anything. My brother Alex is a financial advisor who can help you get rich. Humans and, to an extent, paranormals perceive wealth as power, so you'll need money to conquer the world."

"You make fun of me."

"Yep. It's called teasing."

I entered my number as 'Lily, Savior of His Holiness.' But I used my family's actual names and then taught him how to text. I skipped teaching him how to make calls so I didn't have to answer my phone. "My mom, Ann Marie, will be here in the morning to teach you some stuff. Dad might introduce you to some powerful people. Well, he will if he likes you. I wouldn't hold my breath on that one. He's not fond of too many powerful purebloods."

His eyebrows drew together. "I am your enemy, then?"

Yes. "No. You're my responsibility. My family has strict rules about these things, so don't blow up any human neighborhoods." I tapped my foot. "Maybe just stay here until you learn more about this realm. You're too powerful to be out there alone and ignorant. We can't have you running amok."

"I am a god with excellent control."

"That's not what I meant. You're free to do what you want if you don't break any supernatural or human laws. Be careful about displaying your powers because humans will freak out. If you need to use your magic, then let me know, and we can go to Allure, one of the pocket realms where paranormals live. Start integrating by learning the laws." I motioned to his laptop.

"Very well, I swear to you I will abide by all human and paranormal laws."

The magic contract zinged into place, and I jumped. "Geez, man, take it easy on the contracts. There's no need for all that." Paranormals used magical oaths, which were more binding than paper contracts. If someone was dumb enough to break one, they'd end up in serious trouble when magic extracted its price. I once saw a shifter-elf hybrid end up with permanent green fur, even in her elven form. My dad moved her to an undisclosed location before too many humans saw her. Since then, I avoided making contracts out of sheer terror of what would happen if I broke it.

"You saved my life tonight, Lily. I owe you the same in return. I swear I will protect you and yours and always be available if you need me."

"Damn it, Cavil!" I snapped when the magical contract zinged me. "Knock it off."

His eyes sparkled with malice. Yeah. He knew exactly how uncomfortable the contracts made me. "I swear...."

"Oh, hell no." I cut him off and zipped toward the door. "My house is the one you can see from your backyard, so if you need anything, send a text, and I'll be right over. If you figure out how to circumvent the wards with your massive godly powers and come to visit, stay on the path."

"I swear I'll stay on the paths around your house and only stray off them when necessary." The contract zinged into place.

I raced out the door. "Nope."

"I like this teasing," he called after me.

CHAPTER THREE

I'D WORKED IN A variety of toxic workplaces. While navigating the impossible rules and control-freak bosses, I discovered humans are amazing creatures. They could be the most loving, kind, caring, and helpful beings. Or they could be the most dismissive, cruel, uncaring, and violent beings. Sometimes, those two things were true at the same time. Don't get me wrong, paranormals were often the same way. But they didn't hide their bad sides like humans did. Humans are masters at hiding their evil side.

Nowhere was the contradiction more evident than inside the cubical farm where I worked. The place was even more toxic than retail, and I didn't think that was possible after my stint at a local department store.

My coworkers were upstanding citizens who read bedtime stories to their children, prayed, and helped their neighbors. Then they went to work and found the most cruel, passive-aggressive ways to be awful to each other. It made me feel less bad about my nature. Though, unlike them, I didn't have to convince myself that I didn't have an evil side, being a vampire and all.

A smile spread across my face when the elevator dinged on the floor where I worked. I couldn't wait to see what drama the day would bring.

As I rounded the corner, my boss stepped out of his office. I clenched my fists to keep myself from rubbing my hands together in glee. "Good morning, Kevin."

"You're late."

I faked a frown. "I'm ten minutes early."

"When your shift starts at eight, you should be at your desk at seven forty-five."

I hung my head to hide the excitement in my eyes. "Sorry. Talking to God kept me up late." I left out the 'a' before God. Humans appreciated people who talked to God, no matter how evil they were on the inside. There was no need to mention I only needed about one sleep period per week. I glanced toward the elevators. "I'll go to HR and report myself."

Kevin held up his hands. "No need. Just be more conscious of the time in the future."

"Thank you. I'll be here on time tomorrow."

Kevin slunk back into his office, and I waded through the cubicle farm toward the one assigned to me. It was hard to hide the wicked glint in my eye. Kevin was a mid-level manager who wielded his power like a sword. He knew damn well that if I took his complaint to HR, he'd be the one in trouble. The workplace was toxic as hell, but the HR department at least tried to do its job. I was so glad I didn't land in that department.

A middle-aged face peeked around the corner as I settled into my workspace. "That was one of your best yet."

I put my purse away. I didn't carry it anywhere except for work. It helped me appear more human but a pain in the ass when I had to fight. At least I had a place to put two defensive potions and the pack of gum Maria gave me to keep my fangs clean. "Good morning, Susan. How'd it go last night?"

Susan was a half-human, half-mage with a touch of spirit power. She thought she was human and often called herself a psychic medium. As a result, my presence didn't freak her out like it did everyone else in the office. Watching her try to figure out why the other employees steered clear of me was hilarious. A side-effect of my ever-present dark magical aura. She thought I was a 'nice young lady.' Heh.

She grinned. "The channel is growing. I just hit fifty thousand subscribers, so hopefully..." she trailed off.

"Hopefully soon," I said as I turned on my computer. Like most toxic workplace victims, Susan needed her job to make ends meet. Especially since she was a single mom with a teenager to support. Her human husband died in some war several years before.

The job was just good fun for me. It kept me out of trouble and provided endless entertainment. I was what humans called a trust fund baby. Sort of. My adoptive parents, some of the oldest supernatural creatures on the planet, acquired a fortune over the years. When Alex and I came of age, they hooked us up with trust funds worth millions.

She didn't deserve the stress of working in a toxic environment just because life had dealt her a shitty hand, so I slipped her money every chance I could. I'd often use a throwaway account to donate to her live streams. Sometimes, I'd go fluid and drop a few hundred on her doorstep and then sympathize with her when she couldn't figure out why the camera on her doorbell didn't pick up the mystery person.

I settled into my desk and started the mind-numbingly boring work of going over spreadsheets and creating reports from a financial database. The boredom was a great job perk. It allowed me to tune my sensitive ears into conversations throughout the cube farm.

The IT department was having a staff meeting in the far corner. They kept to themselves and were less toxic than the other departments, so I tuned them out.

One of the girl gangs congregated in a cubicle. I tried not to bounce in my chair as I tuned out the background noise to hear them better. The office gang leader was Kevin's favorite and got away with more than most employees. Other than me. Kevin showed a bit of intelligence by fearing me. The favoritism caused massive resentment, but no one said anything because they'd lose their job if they did. Like I said, it was excellent entertainment.

"I heard they're going to lay off half the workforce. It doesn't apply to me, of course, but you two should worry," she said in her haughty voice. *"Creepy Lily will probably be the first to go."*

"Have you seen what she's wearing today? It's so bland," another woman said.

"She was late today. I don't know why Kevin keeps her around unless she provides...other services."

I snorted, then covered it up with a cough. If he made a move on me, I'd eat that sniveling little weasel for breakfast. Literally.

Across the room, a hotheaded middle manager stomped from her office, so I turned my attention to her. She slammed a thick report on her assistant's desk. *"There's an improper use of a comma on page six. Redo the whole report and try to pay more attention to detail. If you don't start doing a better job, we'll have to discuss the terms of your employment."*

The place was a goldmine. That day, I heard two supervisors steal the credit for their employees' work and witnessed someone who'd only been there a week walk out. Then, when I thought I'd soaked up all the toxicity the office could provide, a guy tried to restock his staples and got bullied by two supply gatekeepers. It was a great day.

Until my phone buzzed half an hour before quitting time.

I pulled the drawer out an inch and peeked in case Cavil needed help. Everyone else knew I couldn't answer my phone in the toxic workplace. It was often grounds for immediate termination. I'd already received one warning, and that's all Kevin had ever given before firing people.

My stomach fell when I saw my brother's name. I yanked the phone out of the drawer, a little sad that I would lose the job. I'd miss the entertainment, but family came first.

Alex: I need backup ASAP.

Me: Where?

Alex: Heading your way. ETA ten minutes.

I didn't have to pack up my desk because I didn't bring a single personal item to work. One always had to be prepared for a good firing.

Heart pounding, I raced into Kevin's office. "I need to go. Family emergency."

He crossed his arms. "How did you learn of this family emergency?"

"Yeah, yeah. No using phones at work and no leaving early without prior approval. I broke the rules. You don't care why. I'm fired. This isn't my first rodeo, Kev." My eyes swept over his pinched face. "Although, I hope you keep up your stellar micromanaging and pettiness. It's great fun." I swept out of the building without looking back. I'd miss Susan, but there was always another toxic workplace.

With adrenaline coursing through me, it took a lot of concentration to walk at human speed. Alex could take care of himself, but my protective instincts urged me to get to him fast.

When my parents adopted him, he was a puny seven-year-old kid. He had bruises from head to toe and was so meek that he'd cower if we looked at him the wrong way. Mom worked for six months to put his body back together. Then, she and Dad spent the next few years working on the emotional issues. It broke my heart to watch it unfold. He was such a sweet kid that I couldn't help but become attached to him. It also made my protective instincts kick into overdrive. They'd never eased.

I spotted Alex a block away, moving at a brisk pace in my direction. His investment firm wasn't far from my current job, but he often worked from home. He didn't tell me he was coming downtown that morning.

I scanned the street for trouble but didn't see anyone. As far as cities went, downtown Boise wasn't that big, but there were several places to hide. I waited for the light, crossed the street, and slid into a doorway. He walked past me without looking and veered into a coffee shop on the corner. It didn't take long before two purebloods passed. Then two more, and two more.

Alex popped out the side door after all six entered the building.

I caught up to him, and we headed toward the parking garage. "What's their deal?"

He pushed his glasses up his nose. "I don't know what they want. They've been following me all day."

I glanced back as they emerged and scanned the street. "There's six of them moving in pairs. Do you think they're with those guys from the bar?"

"I don't know."

"You didn't read them?"

"I'm not an amateur. They want a new mental mage and concluded I qualified for whatever they're scheming. Though they weren't sure what that is."

My heart skipped a beat. Alex wasn't just my baby brother, but my best friend. I'd kill or die for him. "Over my dead body."

He snorted. "Says the vampire. Aren't you already dead?"

"Ha ha. This is serious." Although humans believed vampires were the undead, we weren't. Vampires were created by infecting humans with a magical virus stored in our fangs that we could release at will. It caused the person to get sick and bleed a lot. From what I heard, the transition was hell, but no one who died in the process came back to life. "They need a lesson in hybrid etiquette."

"Agreed."

We took the stairs of the parking garage and turned on our supernatural speed. I'd parked on the third floor, but we went to the fourth. That way, we could take care of them and make a quick getaway.

When we got to the top of the stairs, I went fluid. Cars whizzed by as I headed toward a truck big enough to provide a shadow in broad daylight.

I wrapped it around me while Alex sauntered down the center, pretending to be oblivious.

The two guys rounded the corner. One was a bobcat shifter, the other a mid-level witch. I listened for potions sloshing, but he didn't have any, meaning he wasn't an alchemy witch but one who used the magic in the air to weave spells. That was an advantage for us because it took more time than slinging a potion.

The other four filed in at the other end of the garage. Two mages and two more shifters.

Alex moved to the driver's side of a random car and pretended to unlock it. A shifter slunk my way while the witch wove a spell.

I leaned out enough to see. The cat crouched low, his heartbeat abnormally fast. I fought not to sneeze when the stench of body odor, adrenaline, decay, and a hint of sulfur assaulted my nose. I spotted a discarded lighter, picked it up, and chucked it to the other end of the garage.

The four guys on that end froze.

Taking advantage of the distraction, I hopped over a car. My elbow came down on the shifter's head. He hit the ground with a 'thud' as I landed in a crouch.

I tiptoed around the guy and leaned out to see the witch. He continued to weave his spell. Human-ranged hearing was awful, so he didn't hear his buddy go down.

A car started up somewhere behind me, and his head twisted in my direction.

I jerked back at vampire speed, then poked my head up to see through the windows.

A flash of blue out of the corner of my eye told me Alex was on the move.

I zipped around the car in time to see his hands morph into massive paws. He clapped the witch on both sides of the head, claws out. The guy slumped to the floor.

My head snapped to the four guys on the other end to see if they heard the commotion.

They raced toward us.

I kicked off my shoes and flipped my fangs out. Six-inch claws grew from my hands and feet. A red sheen covered my vision. I went fluid, aiming for the two shifters, stabbed them both in the stomach, then banged their heads together when they bent over in pain.

A burning sensation touched my mind. Alex's mental magic. I peeked around the pickup in time to see the two mages melt to the concrete floor.

Alex came around the corner, an amber glow in his eyes. "Did you kill them?"

I retracted my fangs and claws and went back to get my shoes. "No. They'll heal."

We placed all six of them in a supply closet next to the stairs. I glanced back at the bloodstains on the ground. Nothing I could do about that. "Let's get out of here."

We didn't speak again until we were trapped at a stoplight in rush hour traffic. I glanced in the rearview mirror to make sure no one was following us or acting strange. Being stuck at a stoplight meant we couldn't escape if attacked. It made me twitchy.

Alex cleared his throat. "I got a ride downtown with Mom and planned to ride home with you. Those guys followed me into the office when she dropped me off. They were still in the lobby when I left, so I did a quick scan of their minds and learned they wanted to kidnap me."

I raised a finger from the steering wheel. "I told you they were after you. What do you think that's about?"

Alex swept a hand through his mop of brown hair. "They thought it would be an easy grab and go."

I tapped the steering wheel. "So what? They thought you were weak because you're a hybrid? Or are they so used to getting their own way they didn't consider you'd fight back?"

"I don't know. They had a singular focus."

"And you didn't try to find out what it was? Did you use your magic sight?"

"I'm not stupid. I tried to find out, and yes, I used my magic sight. They looked off, but I can't explain how." He tapped his leg. "Let's head to Mom and Dad's house. Maybe they know what's going on."

CHAPTER FOUR

OUR PARENTS LIVED IN a large ranch-style house a few miles from ours. Instead of leasing their land to hybrid farmers like I did, they planted tall trees, giving them a windbreak and plenty of privacy. The only opening in the trees was the driveway. It looked like a boring, ordinary rural house. They even had animals.

Since Dad oozed predator and animals naturally feared him, Mom had to spell each one to accept him, which caused them to like him more than the rest of us. He loved it and treated them with so much care they'd become spoiled. Even the cows.

I'd never tell him, but I thought he used caring for the farm animals to compensate for his beloved shifters.

Mom's wards pinged as we drove through. I steered my van down the wide gravel driveway that separated the house and barn. The distance from the road gave them plenty of time to prepare for an attack if the heavy wards failed, which they wouldn't. They were paranoid and prepared for anything.

I slipped out of my van and bent down to pet the two golden retrievers who bounded up, big smiles on their faces. The garage was wide open, exposing a riding lawn mower, a wood chipper, and other equipment a person living in the country needed. Dad wasn't inside, so we headed to the house, the two dogs at our sides.

Alex and the retrievers went straight to the kitchen, where Mom hummed as she made dinner. I stopped in the entryway and inhaled the comforting smell of home. For the first twelve years of my life, my authoritarian mother shuffled me from one place to another, then dumped me on my asshole father. The night I escaped was the luckiest night of my life. A lone wolf picked me up outside the gates to Allure and took me to Jonas and Ann Marie. They took me in, cleaned me up, and showered me with love and understanding. The smell of their house always reminded me of safety and comfort. Of unconditional love.

Mom stood at the counter chopping vegetables while a couple of pots boiled on the stove when I shuffled into the kitchen. "Your night to cook, eh?" I asked as she kissed my cheek.

"Your dad's working on that old car, so I let him be."

I leaned against the counter. "No sh...kidding? Why?"

She gave me the mom look. Nothing got past her, especially almost cussing. "He's got a lot on his plate. We've been in negotiations with the Queen of Ahl. She wants to bring the hybrids into the Coalition. There's trouble in paradise, and she's searching for allies."

Allure was located north of where the hybrids had settled in Boise. If something big *was* going down in the pocket, why were so many purebloods in the area? "What kind of trouble?" I tried to sound casual, but my heart pounded out of my chest at becoming part of the Coalition.

Alex tried to snatch a piece of cucumber, and Mom slapped his hand. "Not the kind you need to concern yourself with. Your little hideout is far away from the action. Are you staying for dinner?"

"Yes," Alex answered.

I grinned. "We'd love to. Did you meet the new rescue?"

"I did. I'm still not sure what to think about him. He seems nice enough and is smart. Do I believe he's a god?" She shrugged. "I guess time will tell."

Alex eyed the roast as mom slipped it into the oven. "Cavil's great. He wants to learn as much as possible and has already given me a few valuables to sell to build his wealth."

I climbed onto a barstool at the kitchen island. "Where did he get valuables? He didn't have anything last night."

"He said he visited this realm before and stashed them all over the world. I went into town this afternoon because I needed to get them to auction."

I pulled out my phone to feign disinterest. "Huh."

Dad came in, swiped a hand through his brown hair, and went to wash his hands. As he dried them, a lopsided smile spread across his face. "What's this about?" It was hard to tell that he was one of the most powerful people in the world by looking at him.

I slid off my stool to set the table. "Someone's after Alex."

Alex told them about the guys we left unconscious in the parking garage.

"Interesting." Dad tried to steal a piece of tomato. Mom slapped his hand away. He let out an exaggerated sigh. "Were the four purebloods in the bar the same ones following you today?"

"Different," Alex answered.

"Another First informed me of an uprising against the new queen. He said they like to use mind control mixed with demon magic. The guys after Alex may be part of that."

My spine snapped straight. "How much danger are we in?"

"It's a group of rebels we fought off long ago. There are reports of some purebloods amassing in the city, so use caution. A mage like Alex would be a prize for them. Drake thinks they want to add hybrids to their ranks and requested my help."

"You don't believe him."

"Drake's honorable, but I'd like to avoid coalition politics if I can, and helping him puts me in the center of them."

"So if you don't help, and they somehow get their hooks into Alex? What then?"

"They won't. Both of you are excellent at subversion and skilled fighters. I'm confident you can fight your way out of or escape most situations."

"Alex is right here," my brother said. "Something about their brain patterns isn't right. Mind control fits."

Mom leaned forward. "What do you mean?"

He shook his head. "I don't know exactly. It's like most people have several thoughts in their heads at once. They think about their problems, practice what to say in a situation, worry about their finances and families, or dream of their futures. These guys only focus on the task at hand. I might be reading them wrong, but it's like they can't see past their current goal."

Dad nodded. "It's the mind control monitoring this group uses. You two need to avoid them."

I took a drink of water.

"I mean it, Lily. Until I find out more information, steer clear."

Alex shook his head. "I don't know why you bother. You know she won't listen."

"I don't know why you want me to. I'm the best spy in this family and could track them down in no time."

Mom patted my hand. "Because he cares about you and doesn't want you to put yourself in danger, firefly. You do the same thing to Alex."

Firefly was a nickname she gave me when I was a kid because the only vampire skill I knew was going fluid. I was always zipping around, so Mom gave me a charm that glowed. It helped them keep track of me. "I don't do that to Alex. Okay, maybe I do, but this is different."

Dad sighed. "If you go out looking for them, you text us your location and what you find. If they spot you, get out and don't go back. Do not confront these guys. Clear?"

"Clear."

The ward pinged.

Dad gave Mom a pointed look and headed to the garage.

Alex slid out of his chair. "I'll get it."

Mom washed her hands and turned to me. "Stay here." Her voice didn't leave any room for discussion.

I shrugged. "Sure." I tuned my hearing and concentrated on the front of the house, but the wards made it impossible to hear anything. Mom knew all my tricks.

Alex stumbled back to the kitchen and rubbed his head. "That woman packs a punch."

"Who?"

"Some lady and a dragon are out front."

"Coalition representatives?"

"Probably. I couldn't get into their heads."

I glanced toward the door. "Should we worry?"

"No. Mom knows them. She wouldn't leave the wards if they were a threat."

I went back to my phone. After a few minutes, voices sounded from the garage, and a massive, beat-up man with jet-black hair emerged. He scanned us with his bright green eyes. "Thank you for the dinner invitation, Jonas. Unfortunately, I can't stay. Jenella disappeared with Ann Marie."

Dad stiffened. "Ann Marie won't hurt her."

The man's eyes flipped to me and narrowed.

I was staring, trying to work out what type of magic the guy had. It wasn't quite a dragon, but it wasn't mage, either. I dragged my eyes away.

"I know," the guy said in a slow, measured voice.

Dad brushed past him and placed himself between us. "Meet our youngest children, Lily and Alex. This is one of my oldest friends and the only other First still awake, Drake."

I raised a hand, still trying to get a feel for his magic. "Whazzup?"

Alex elbowed me. "Nice to meet you, Sir First."

The man's lip twitched. "Nice to meet you, Lily and Alex." He turned back to Dad. "Please let me know if you find anything."

Dad shot me a look and followed him out the door.

When Mom returned, she went back to cooking as if the interruption hadn't happened.

I set my phone down. "What is that guy?"

She chuckled. "You'll never get a read on him, so you might as well not try. Like all the Firsts, he's one of a kind, though I don't remember what, exactly."

Dad came back in and took his seat. "Tell me about the new god."

I launched into the story of how I found Cavil.

After we finished our dinner, Alex cleared our plates. "What should we do if the mind-controlled guys come after us again?"

Mom leaned back. "Go home and stay behind your wards. If you can't get home, go to Allure, get a hotel room, and lie low."

"No. We'll be in more danger in Allure."

She shook her head. "You don't know this group. They have a vast network and are not above using demons and other nasty tactics." Mom conjured a ball of white magic. "The Queen showed me this. It neutralizes their current concoction. Absorb it. I'm going to contact the alchemy witches to see if they want my help to develop an immunity potion."

Alex poked at it and then nodded. "Got it."

I did the same, though I doubted I could use the stuff without it turning violent.

"That was the queen out there, and you're going to help her?" My voice sounded higher than normal. "Why?"

"Yes, that was the queen. And I'm going to help her because I made an oath to the first queen that I would. On top of that, I want you to be safe. If that means becoming her BFF, then that's what I'll do."

Alex and I made it home at sunset, and I drifted to the back porch to see if I could spot Cavil and think. Mom threw me for a loop with all her talk about Allure and the Queen. I wanted nothing to do with either of them, but she was an ancient who played the long-game. I knew it was smart to listen to her. Didn't mean I wanted to.

When I didn't see Cavil, I texted I was on my way over. As soon as I sent it, the porch light came on, and his hulking figure emerged from the side door and started across the DMZ. When he got close enough for me to see him, he waved. I couldn't help but smile as I went fluid and appeared at the fence.

Cavil made his way down the path, walking at an even pace. "Why do you have a maze in your field? Is it common in this realm?"

"Not common, no. It's the DMZ. Uh, demilitarized zone. I planted it to keep the previous tenant from shooting us." I waved a hand. "Long story. How goes the empire building?"

"Don't you fucking cross that fence and trample the damn yard, you big oaf!" A small but loud voice came from the base of a nearby tree.

I turned to the gnome I'd rescued from a large plant in a toxic workplace. "Language, Flemming."

"Oh, fuck off, Lily." He pointed a tiny finger at Cavil. "You stay the hell on the paths, and don't be pawing the flowers. I didn't put all that damn work in for you to fuck it up."

My face flushed. "Sorry about that. Flemming learned curse words a couple of months ago."

Cavil grinned. "I've already vowed to stay on the paths, gnome. I will not break it."

"You better fucking not, or I'll kick your ass."

Cavil's gaze settled on my feet, which were, in fact, on the grass.

Flemming threw his arms in the air. "Lily owns the fucking place, scallywag. She can do what she damn well pleases. You can't."

I cleared my throat. "He's got it, Flemming."

He grunted and disappeared into the lawn.

"Sorry about that," I repeated. "He's a rescue and a little overprotective of his domain."

Cavil's eyes met mine. "I thought you were exaggerating when you said you rescued people."

"Nope. He got separated from his wife and kids when they put a parking lot on the land they claimed. He moved into a nearby plant and looked for them at night. That's where I found him. I've been looking for his family, but gnomes are hard to find." I tapped my chin. "The cussing is new. It makes me wonder if he's losing his mind without them."

He nodded as if I had answered a question. "I've learned many laws and cultural norms. I have also begun building my wealth. Your family is helpful."

"That's good to hear. Alex said he was selling some stuff for you, so you'll have some money soon."

"I already have plenty of money, but the sale of the artifacts will help."

My eyes narrowed. "How did you get money?"

"I am a god. Which means I have creation magic. I simply created a bank account."

"You made an oath that you wouldn't break any laws. Last time I checked, counterfeiting money is against the law."

He crossed his arms. "I did not break any laws. I created a bank account and transferred funds from an account in my home realm at a fair exchange rate. According to Jonas, it was a currency exchange. Although, he mentioned I should not do it again because it could draw unwanted attention. Therefore, I am selling some artifacts." He shrugged. "Your brother has already transferred it to another account. No laws say I can't exchange currency from another realm."

Great. Cavil had been with us for one day and already had my dad compromising his morals and my brother laundering money for him. Sort of. The guy would fit in well with the purebloods in the pockets. I eyed his hair. Where it was long and flowing the night before, it was now short on the sides and back, and longer on the top with a messy swoop. I hated it. It made him look like a fashion model or a pro wrestler. "If you say so. And look. You even found time to get an expensive haircut."

"Again, I am a god. I can style my hair." He waved a hand. "I need your help to purchase a home in the pocket of Allure."

"Sorry, Your Holiness, you're out of luck. I don't know much about the pockets or real estate."

"Finding a representative is not the problem. I'd like you to help me pick out a proper place once I do. Something appropriate for a god in this realm."

My heart sank. The guy was weird and had questionable morals, but I kind of liked him. I wanted him to stay around a little longer. "You're moving to Allure?"

"Only part-time. I am already negotiating to buy the farmhouse but would also like one in Allure. It is important for me to establish myself with both humans and powerful paranormals."

"No shit? You move fast." And my parents would probably sell him the farmhouse, too. Butterflies erupted in my stomach at the thought of him living next door, and I tamped them down. Not going there.

"Yes. After my items sell at auction and I find an appropriate representative, I'll send you an electronic message."

I had to make the trek to Allure once per month to release my magic, so I supposed I could do both at the same time. "Okay, I'll go with you. But I need to run an errand while we're there."

"Very well. I swear I will allow you to run your errand and consider your advice about houses."

The magical contract snapped into place. "Damn it, Cavil."

His bright smile was almost worth the unneeded contract. "Good night, Lily." He turned and strode back down the path and through the maze.

"Night." I watched him go and wondered what I got myself into.

CHAPTER FIVE

THE ONE THING I hated about not sleeping often was I couldn't turn off my brain. That night, it kept circling around to the purebloods. I needed to learn more about them. The situation had Mom on edge. And she never bothered worrying about the small stuff. So whatever was happening in Allure was big. Which meant it was a matter of time before it landed on our doorstep, if it hadn't already. The stuff Alex plucked out of their minds confirmed that possibility.

I climbed into my van and shook off the stab of guilt for waiting until Alex went to sleep to do my investigating. I pulled onto the road and headed toward Hooves.

Dale's wife, Darla, stood behind the bar. "Hey, Lily. The usual?"

"Sounds great. Thanks, Darla." I slid onto a barstool. There were only four other patrons, all hybrids.

She poured a vodka tonic. "What brings you out on a Wednesday night?"

"Some purebloods decided it would be a good idea to kidnap Alex."

She snorted. "I bet that went over well."

"About as well as you'd expect." I focused on a woman sitting by herself, tapping on her phone. "A few purebloods were in here last night. I picked up four of them talking about us. One was a vampire. I plan to figure out what's going on."

Darla cursed under her breath. "I told Dale those guys were trouble." She flipped her brown hair over her shoulder. "The vampires usually lurk outside. The other guys have been in a few times over the last month. One even told me I was a disgrace for serving these filthy creatures." She waved a hand toward the patrons.

She was a pureblood moose shifter and, like her natural counterparts, mean as hell. Those guys were lucky to be alive. "That's rude."

"Right? It's not the first time I've been called names since matching with Dale. But in my own bar?" She shook her head. "Pocket people suck."

"They really do." Every time I went to Allure to release my magic, someone harassed me. It was the same story with all hybrids, so we commiserated and wore our resentment like a badge of honor.

Darla wondered off to replace the beers for a couple on a date. I slumped over my drink, thinking about where to go from there. If the purebloods didn't show up, then I had no leads. The city was too big and spread-out to drive around looking for them. Those guys could be anywhere. Though, I'd bet anything Mom and Dad knew more than they told us. They usually did.

I pondered whether I could manipulate Jedediah's goons to help, but dismissed the idea. My biological father was a complete asshat. He'd probably kill his own vampires if I made them help. They were so scared of him they flinched when I called him good ole Jed.

An idea formed, and a smile spread across my face. I finished my drink, slapped a twenty on the counter, and slid out the door.

The North side of Boise, what locals referred to as the North End, was a hodge-podge of updated picture-perfect historic houses, not-so-nice ones, and rentals. Sometimes right next door to each other. They were as eclectic as the people who lived in them. I wasn't super familiar with the area because it was too crowded for my tastes, but I had to admit it held a certain charm. I found the street I was looking for and circled the block until I found a parking spot near the local vampire house.

As a teenager, I convinced Mom to take me there. I had this big idea that they'd help me learn some vampire skills. My teenage brain thought they'd be nicer than the ones in the pockets since the house was in the human world. It did not go as planned.

I expanded my hearing and kept my mage senses on alert as I stepped out of the van and started down the street. A dog barked inside a house as I passed, and the hum of traffic from the street a few blocks away made it hard to tune my hearing. I swung my head from side to side as I walked and wondered if I was making a huge mistake.

Probably. Purebloods were all assholes. And when I went to these vampires for help as a kid, they threw me out on my ass and told me to never come back. The fact I was considering it told me I was running on instinct rather than logic. But I wasn't a kid anymore, so if they told me to get lost, I wouldn't take their rejection personally. I'd leave and figure something else out.

I stopped at the edge of the property and felt for wards. Finding none, I continued up the sidewalk to the pristine western colonial-style house. The dark blue color and white accents were fresh. As was the landscaping. It made me hesitate. I didn't feel a stabbing in my chest, so I wasn't sure if they still lived there. If not, the humans who bought the house would probably call the police for knocking on their door in the middle of the night.

I took a deep breath, stretched out a shaky hand, and rang the doorbell.

The door swung open, and a pair of dark eyes swept over me. "We're not ready to receive new vampires just yet."

The same guy who threw me out before, and not the housemaster. I shifted my weight. "Good. Because I'm not interested in joining your house. Have you guys noticed all the purebloods in the area lately?"

He brushed his jet-black hair out of his face, but didn't respond.

"Right. So, I'm Lily, Jonas and Ann Marie's daughter. I wondered if Roman would be interested in helping me gather information on them."

He cocked his head. "I will ask him. Should he agree, he will be in contact with you." He slammed the door in my face.

"Great. Thanks."

I sat in my van for a few minutes, considering what to do next. The non-answer from the vampires was better than I'd expected, but I couldn't count on them. I had no leads, no help, and no idea what to do next. And my instincts still screamed at me. So I headed back to the bar. I'd have to hope some would show up so I could follow them.

I sat across the street and watched. After a couple of hours, I was bored and ready to give up and go home. No cars had come or gone in over an hour, and there were only four in the parking lot. As I turned the key in the ignition, two guys turning the corner caught my attention. Both weak mages. Bingo. I watched them as they jumped into a car parked on the adjacent street.

I waited for them to turn the corner before I followed. They went a few miles and pulled into the parking lot of a building with a sign that read, 'Integrated Supply Co.' I drove by without looking and parked in a shopping center down the street.

A prickle on the back of my neck started as soon as I stepped out of the van. I leaned against the driver's side door, crossed my arms, and scanned the street. I spotted a white dragon perched on a roof. As soon as I caught a quick glimpse, he disappeared. I couldn't sense or see him, so I wondered if I'd imagined it.

The thought scattered when a shadow crept in front of the darkened storefront.

I focused on it. When it twitched, I went fluid and was across the parking lot in the blink of an eye. I punched the guy in the temple with my full strength. He slumped to the ground, unconscious. It would only last a minute or two, so I used my vampire strength to lift Jedediah's goon into a fireman's carry and dumped him in the back of the van. Mom spelled it to restrain volatile strays until we could convince them they were safe. She even figured out a way to make it work on vampires. Though, until that moment, I never knew why. Mom always thought ahead.

Problem solved, I went fluid and stopped at the edge of the supply company parking lot. I crouched behind a bush and pulled the shadows around myself.

Cars were parked in the parking lot, but not so many to draw attention. It wasn't unusual for humans to work late. Most of them worked themselves to death out of necessity or greed. But they usually cleared out long before midnight. And purebloods wouldn't be caught dead working in a human business. I stayed in the shadows as I crept around the back. A witch leaned against the wall, smoking next to an open door.

A shifter stuck his head out. "Get in here and finish your report so we can get some sleep."

The witch stomped out what looked like a joint and followed. "Yeah, yeah. I'm coming."

He kicked the wedge out of the door as he went in. It bounced off the stoop and flipped back. I went fluid and lodged the tip in the door before it closed, then returned to my hiding spot and settled in to wait.

When only two cars remained in the lot, I made my move. I didn't want to wait until they were all gone in case they had an alarm. I went fluid to the corner of the building and slunk down the brick toward the door.

A car started in the front lot.

I froze. Then slunk further into the shadows and pulled them closer. I tuned my hearing to the front of the building. Several voices came from that direction, but I couldn't quite make out what they were saying because of the road noise. Filtering it out would take too long, so I tiptoed toward the door, cracked it open, and peered in.

The hallway was dark. I stretched my ears.

Someone typed on a loud keyboard while two men talked in the front lobby. I made sure the wedge was in place and slipped inside, keeping my footsteps as light as possible. The hall ran straight down the center of the building with two doors on each side. From where I stood, it looked like the front half was wide open. None of the office doors were closed, so I started on the one on my right. It was a small office with an old pressboard desk and not much else. Not even a computer. I darted to the next office and found the same thing.

A footstep scuffed against the carpet in the hall, so I scooted back into the shadows. I'd forgotten to keep my ears tuned in on the guys. Dang it. I needed to learn how to be a better vampire if I was going to spy.

I'd spent years teaching myself to be less intimidating and more unassuming, so the hybrid kids we picked up didn't think I was after a meal. Not that I needed blood. It wasn't a requirement for me, like every other vampire on the planet. Mom thought my mage abilities had something to do with that. Dad wasn't so sure, but never gave me an alternative theory. Either way, I tried to stay away from the stuff because I had no desire to head down that path. It led to the need to join a house and hang out with other vampires. No thanks.

The footsteps went into the office next door. A screech from a filing cabinet opening came from the office, then another when it closed. The person dragged his feet as he moved back to the front area.

"Let's get out of here," a high-pitched male voice said.

"Finally," said a deeper one.

The front door opened and closed, and a key in the lock clicked.

I peeked out and saw the green light on the building's alarm. And breathed a sigh of relief. They didn't set it.

I waited for their car to start before I tiptoed to the next office.

There were two desks, each with a closed laptop on them. I pulled off my backpack and shoved them in it, then opened the first drawer of the filing cabinet and thumbed through the files. There were too many to take, so I had to be selective. The second drawer was only half full. It was labeled 'financial,' so I skipped it.

The last two drawers were empty. Apparently, they didn't care if the cabinet was top-heavy and could fall over. I once witnessed a woman almost get crushed in a toxic workplace that had similar safety standards. She got fired.

I stuffed files in my backpack and checked the last office. There were more laptops and one desktop computer. I rummaged through the building until I found a box and filled it. The desktop computer was too bulky to carry, so I had to leave it. Even the box would be a problem if I had to fight, but it was worth the risk. I slipped out the back door, removed the wedge, and made sure the door was closed. Heart pounding, I went fluid all the way back to the edge of the shopping center where I'd parked.

I came to a sudden stop when a needling stabbed through my chest. I slunk into the shadows and set down the box. The feeling meant a blood relation was nearby, and I didn't want to get ambushed by good ole Jed.

Closing my eyes, I examined the sensation. It wasn't very strong like it was when my mother or Jed were close. I was only aware of a handful of blood relations, so it could be an uncle or cousin. I took a deep breath, adjusted my backpack, grabbed the box, and continued at a brisk human pace.

Roman, the House Master I tried to recruit, stood beside my van.

I went around to the back and pushed the button to open the hatch. "Roman."

"Hello."

"Are you going to help me with the purebloods or throw me out on my ass again?" When I was a kid, the dark-haired man who answered the door earlier handled that. Mom hit him with some nasty magic and dragged me away as I sobbed. That was the day I decided to avoid blood relations because they all sucked. I hadn't had a single desire to get to know any of them since.

Jed's goon bounded out the back and went fluid, no doubt trying to get away from me. I threw the box and backpack in and pushed the button to close it. And waited. And waited some more. Not the badass statement I was going for. I missed my old van, where I could slam the back for dramatic effect. The button push-wait was awkward.

Roman raised an eyebrow.

I raised mine back.

When the latch clicked, he spoke. "I was unaware another vampire had claimed this territory and am here to inform you of my plans to reestablish a house, as is vampire custom."

I gave him a thumbs-up as I pushed past him. "Yay, you. Don't prey on law-abiding humans or hybrids, and I won't kill you. Did you get my message?"

He answered with a dramatic sigh. "Yes. And I will help you, but understand that I have only begun the recruiting process to reestablish my house." He paused. "As for your threat, I sense your enormous potential, young one. However, I doubt an attempt on my life would turn out well for you. I could simply restrain you outside and wait for daylight."

His face remained expressionless as he spoke. The only other person I'd ever seen do that was Jed. I wasn't sure what to think about the guy. As an ancient, he *was* powerful enough that I wouldn't be successful in killing him on my own. But I was confident my family as a unit could take him and his vampires out if needed.

Then there was the family connection. I hadn't felt it as a kid. I was so scared of Jed and paranoid that I always scanned for that sensation back then. But it didn't show up either time I went to his house, and I wondered why. Not that I'd ask him. He'd probably tell me, and that scared the shit out of me more than the sensation did.

I rested my hand on the door. "Daylight isn't a problem for me because I'm not quite a vampire. You really don't want me to use my other skills on you. So, either accept my terms or piss off. Either way, I'm done with this fun little conversation."

Two cars I'd seen at the supply business zoomed by on the street. I went fluid and ducked into the shadows. Roman followed, only he did both much better than me. If I didn't have that damn sensation in my chest, I would never have known he was there.

As soon as they passed, I hopped into the van and pushed the button to start it. The passenger door opened, and Roman slid in and buckled his seatbelt. "No need to be rude. Folami, my second, said you requested our help. I only wish to speak to you about the territory and your proposal."

I pulled out of the parking lot and turned in the opposite direction of the supply store. "If you can't find your way home from Parma, get out now because I'm not a taxi service."

If he stayed, I'd dump him on Cavil and watch the fun ensue. I didn't know what would happen when an ancient vampire clashed with a supposed god, but I was willing to find out.

"That vampire you held captive. He was not a member of your house?"

"No. He's a spy for another vampire who thinks he can own me."

Roman's face scrunched. "You should have either stolen him or killed him. You may regret that mistake in the future."

"No thanks. I don't want a house. And I've traveled down the killing road before. Good ole Jed will just send someone else. Besides, that guy is easy to spot and terrified of me, so he's the best option."

"Who is Goodall Jed?"

"Good. Old. Jed. As in Jedediah, Prince of Vampires and asshole supreme."

Roman stiffened. "Ah. Prince Jedediah."

I wasn't sure how much to tell Roman about my heritage. No way I wanted to get on the Vampire Queen's radar, and I was positive he was tied to her. All vampires were. I heard some horror stories about her over the years. One particular story was how she delt with minor infractions by cutting off limbs and locking vampires in a freezer until they grew back. I couldn't imagine what she would do to a hybrid abomination like me. "Yes."

"And why is he spying on you?"

"Because I won't talk to him."

"Why not? It is customary for a house leader to bring in a rogue vampire. Which is another reason I approached you."

"I'm not a rogue vampire, nor am I interested in joining a house, least of all Jed's." Been there, done that, blew it up. "Besides, you had your chance to help me when I was a kid, and you threw me out on my ass. I don't need you or any other vampire now."

Roman frowned. "I do not recall a half-breed approaching me to join my house."

The stab of rejection hurt. He wasn't the one who threw me out, but nothing happened in a vampire house without the master knowing. When I approached him, it was less than a year after my parents adopted me. They had their hands full with their new kid, and I was thirsty for knowledge. I spent weeks working up the courage to approach Roman's house. "Doesn't matter."

"I apologize. That was very insensitive. I would be glad to take you in now."

"That'll be a no for me. Vampires have been awful to me my whole life, including the dude who answered your door. I'm not interested in being taunted and rejected. Nor am I a weak teenager anymore. I'm better off sticking with my family."

"I am sorry for that, Liliana. Had I known you visited, I would have provided you with proper support. We are blood-related, after all."

"My name's Lily," I snapped. "And how the hell do you know we're blood-related?"

"Do you not have the ability to sense blood relations yet? I would have thought you'd develop the skill as soon as you were turned."

"You need to catch up with the times, Roman. I'm a born vampire."

"Impossible. There hasn't been a natural-born vampire in over three thousand years."

"If you say so."

"What were you doing at that supply store?"

The tension in my shoulders drained at the change of subject. "Gathering information. Someone tried to kidnap a member of my adopted family, and I can't let that stand."

"So, you were spying."

"Yep."

He turned his head to gaze out the window as I pulled onto the freeway. "I wish to help you in any way I can, even if you are not a member of my house."

My eyes narrowed. "Why?"

"Don't be so paranoid. I do not wish you harm or ill will. Since this territory rightfully belongs to me, I only want to protect it. I cannot do that without ensuring every vampire in it behaves."

"You gave up the right to the territory when you shut down your house and denied me help. I claimed it, so it's legally mine." For the first twelve years of my life, my biological mother drilled coalition laws into my head. I was an expert on them. "You could fight me for it, or we can negotiate. Your call."

Roman threw his head back and laughed. "You are quite entertaining with all your blustering. I shall enjoy getting to know you. Let the negotiations begin."

CHAPTER SIX

IT WASN'T UNTIL THE tires crunched on the gravel driveway of the farmhouse that I realized I may have made a mistake. First, it was super late, and I knew nothing about Cavil or his sleeping habits. Second, I wasn't sure he'd let us negotiate there. I should have sent a text or something.

I exhaled when we rounded the bend, and the farmhouse was lit up like Christmas. The power bill would be astronomical. Not that it was my problem.

I raised my hand to knock on the door, and it swung open, revealing a smiling Cavil. "What a pleasant surprise." His face turned to stone when he spotted Roman lurking in the shadows by the van. "That is not another stray."

Cavil wore only a tight pair of sweatpants, leaving his massive chest bare. I ignored the heat that lit up my body at the sight, swallowed, and tried to concentrate on his face. It was not easy. "Uh. No. Uh, Cavil, this is Roman, the local vampire House Master. Roman, meet Cavil. Can we come in?"

Cavil straightened to his full height and crossed his arms. His sheer power almost blew me off the porch. "What does the local House Master want with me?"

I only knew him for a day, but it never crossed my mind that he could be so cold. His power was obvious, but until then, he'd been curious and playful. The scary side sent more heat through my body. I cleared my throat. "As hot as all that power makes you, he's not here for you. It's me he wants. We need a neutral place to work through some negotiations."

He didn't budge. "Speak, vampire."

Roman glided to my side and offered an old-fashioned bow. "My apologies for invading your space. I was unaware a god had moved to the area. I'm attempting to reestablish my house after a sabbatical, you see. Lily refused the offer to join my house and said she claimed the area. To avoid bloodshed, we have agreed to negotiate."

Cavil's stony face turned to me.

I threw up my hands. "You purebloods have giant sticks up your asses about social protocols. All the posturing is exhausting, so just save some time and either let us in or say no. Either is fine with me."

A blinding smile lit his face. "You may negotiate here. I will attend to learn more about the customs of this realm."

I drooled a little when his muscles shifted, and he stepped out of the way and motioned for us to pass.

Roman went first, and I followed, ignoring the tingle between my shoulder blades. Jed's goon was back at his spying gig. The tingle disappeared when the hair on the back of my neck stood up as Cavil moved behind me.

He pointed toward the tattered living room. "We will negotiate in there."

I curled into a large recliner that reeked of cigar smoke and gun oil while Roman perched on the couch. Cavil threw on a gray T-shirt that matched his sweats and sprawled on the love seat.

Roman cleared his throat. "I would like to be honest with you. My house currently has one other vampire, Folami. He has been by my side for centuries and was under orders to reject new vampires who showed up at my door. I do not wish to establish a large house, nor do I have any desire to move into a pocket."

"Except I'm not a new vampire. As I said before, I was born this way. When I came to you for help, I was barely a teenager, and my mage magic was at war with my vampire side. On top of that, my biological family had already tried to kill me, so it took every ounce of courage I had to approach you. The only thing I needed from you was some guidance. My adoptive parents were not comfortable teaching me, though they tried. I hoped you'd help. You rejected me. I figured it out. End of story. I'm not joining your house, so take that off the table. But I'm willing to negotiate an alliance."

The glint in his eye told me he still didn't believe my story. "Very well. I propose we share information. When I felt the familial bond, I thought you were one of my human descendants who got turned at some point. But even if you are a born vampire like you claim, it doesn't change the fact that you are family. I suspect through my sister. I do not shun family. Nor will I force you into the vampire network against your will. However, you must understand if the queen asks about you, I cannot lie."

His admission that he was the brother of the Vampire Queen meant he was my great-uncle. I made a mental note of the difference in the prickling sensations. "She won't. I'm the dirty little secret they want to sweep under the rug, so you don't have to worry about that. Here's what I propose. You establish your house in Boise, and I'll stay out here unless I go to my favorite bar or have business there. Let's agree to allow each other to cross the boundaries as needed and work together if there's a threat."

Roman sniffed. "Well, you see. That will not work for me. Vampire law clearly states only one house is allowed within a certain radius of a pocket. If we base it on the size of pocket of Allure, then this area is still mine...."

I tuned him out. My brain couldn't handle the long-winded speech. When he was done, I rubbed my temples and ignored Cavil's blinding smile. "There's a large hybrid community in Boise. If you establish a house here, you'll need to become part of it."

He tapped his chin. "I will discuss that with Jonas the First, of course. But that does not solve our dispute."

In the end, we agreed that we'd work together. He insisted on making me an honorary member of his house to comply with the laws and explained for ten minutes that honorary members were not under the authority of the Housemaster but recognized as close allies.

I agreed to shut him up.

With the negotiations complete, I filled him in on the purebloods in the area and Alex's would-be abductors. I also asked him to help me spy. The idea thrilled Roman.

Cavil offered to transport him home with magic, and I was more than happy to dump that responsibility on him. They disappeared as I headed to my van.

Cavil reappeared before I could open the door.

I jumped at his sudden reappearance. "That was fast."

"I am a god. Which means I can go anywhere in the world in the blink of an eye."

"I see that. Do you think you can get into the pockets that way?"

"They are heavily warded, so I'm not sure. Nor will I try without proper clearance."

"Then we better take the van when you house hunt. Make sure you have the proper paperwork to get through the gates. My dad can help you with that."

"Thank you for the advice. I will contact Jonas."

An awkward silence followed.

I stood by my car. He stood at the base of the steps. When our eyes met, a jolt of lightning went through me. Nope. Not going there. I jerked the door open. "Good night, Cavil."

"Good night, Lily." The deep rumble of his voice gave me chills. I needed to do something about my dry spell.

When I got home, I dragged the loot into the house. Alex was still asleep, so I headed straight to my office on the first floor. I didn't want to connect the laptops to my Wi-Fi. No telling what kind of nasty stuff was on them. We had people who could safely extract the information, so I set them aside and dug out the paper files.

It took a few hours. Most of it was boring low-level administrative stuff. I examined an organizational chart, then set it aside and went over their dossiers on a few hybrids they planned to recruit, Alex being one of them.

From what I gathered, their goal was to break up the Coalition and install some idiot as king. Then, they planned world domination. I rolled my eyes at that. Every group of sycophants to exist wanted world domination. It never worked out for them. You'd think they'd take the hint, but no.

I didn't give a damn about the Coalition or their leaders. I only cared about what they wanted with the hybrids. And what lengths they'd go to get Alex.

The papers didn't give me that information. But they revealed their plans to invade the hybrids and turn us all into slaves. "They think we're weak," I said out loud. "They think they can just come in here, take over, and enslave us without a fight."

I packed it up to take to my parents. They needed the information more than me. Maybe Roman could help them spy since he was much better at using his vampire skills. I'd tag along and see if I could learn a few things from him.

That decided, I scrolled through job listings to find another toxic workplace. Retail was always an option. Stores were infamous for being awful to their employees. Plus, I could freak the customers out with my creepy essence. That was always good fun.

I filled out an application, then hesitated. Until I knew Alex was safe, I'd worry about him while at work. And that would suck all the fun out of it.

I deleted the application.

Chapter Seven

The property wards pinged just before dawn. I stretched and shuffled to a small office off the kitchen to view the monitors. The human security monitors sat on the right, and the magical monitors on the left. I scanned the cameras first and then activated the observation spell.

Alex skidded through the door wearing only his boxer briefs, his mop of brown hair a tangled mess from sleeping. "It's Jedediah."

Sure enough. An expensive black SUV sat at the end of the driveway. My biological father stood at the gate, his hand against the ward, his dark hair slicked back. He brushed off his perfectly tailored suit and said something to the four vampires fanned out behind him. His spy stood among them. I turned on the sound in time to hear Jed ask, "How much do you suppose these wards cost her?"

Spy guy stood with his hands clasped behind his back. "I believe the sorceress, Ann Marie, set them for free."

Jed leaned forward. "I did not know Ann Marie had magic that works on vampires. It is very rare." He stepped back and eyed the house. "Liliana! I only wish to talk to you. I would not be here if it wasn't important."

Alex snorted. "Important for who?"

I folded my arms to hide the shaking. "Him. I'm pretty sure he thinks the entire world revolves around him."

Alex reached over and turned on the speaker. "Hey, Jed. I know you're incapable of taking a hint, but Lily has nothing to say to you. Leave."

I crossed my arms and leaned against the wall as the vampires talked quietly amongst themselves. My stomach turned at the thought that he showed up. His goons were weaker than me, so they bothered me about as much as flies buzzing around my head. Jed's presence felt more like a rattlesnake getting ready to strike. It stirred up all kinds of memories I didn't want to think about. The guy was bad news. He wanted something from me, and I was positive whatever it was would be awful.

Jed lowered his head. "Servant, please tell my daughter I want to make amends." He dropped an envelope on the ground. "That is a very exclusive dinner invitation. Your attendance is required." He hopped into the back of the SUV. The tires squealed as they sped away.

He left the spy.

Alex stomped toward the kitchen. "Are you okay, Lily?"

I trailed behind him. "I'd be better if you put some clothes on. Preferably clean."

He yanked the coffee out of the pantry and shot me a look. "This is serious."

"No shit." My stomach tried to revolt, and I swallowed a few times, then clenched my jaw to keep from dumping my emotional crap on Alex. He had enough trauma of his own and didn't need to carry mine. "I need to figure out how to get rid of him. We can't have him following us around, especially since that group of idiots is after you."

"He thinks I'm your servant. I could talk to him. Maybe he'll go away." He pointed toward the front door. "Maybe start with reading that note."

"Jed's a housemaster and a prince. I'm pretty sure he thinks everyone is his servant. And no, I'm not sending you to deal with my personal shit. Knowing him, he'd take you hostage to draw me out."

"Send Dad. Nobody screws with him."

True. As a First, most purebloods steered clear of our dad. He presented himself as a typical rural family man to the humans, but paranormals could feel his power. Humans would shit their pants if they knew what lurked under all that 'awe shucks' and 'yes, ma'am.' "I'll think about it."

I wiped my sweaty hands on my pants and swallowed back bile as I stared down at the dinner invitation. The date was in three weeks at an address in Allure. I pulled out my phone, went on the maginet and searched for it. When I found it, my knees went weak. I lowered myself into a chair and ran a hand through my hair. This was bad. On a scale from one to ten, it was a thousand. The dinner was at the Vampire Queen's house.

I glanced at the stairs. Alex was working, so I didn't want to disturb him. But I needed to talk to someone. If there was one thing our parents taught us, it was that keeping our emotions bottled up was a waste of time. I stuffed the invitation in my pocket, gathered the stuff I took from that office, and headed to my parent's house.

I found Mom in front, working in a flower garden. She used magic instead of her hands, but she loved playing the part of the human gardener. When I got out of the van, she pulled off her clean gloves and adjusted her big floppy hat. "What brings you here this morning?"

"I stole a bunch of stuff from those purebloods. I thought you'd like to see it."

"That was fast."

I pulled out the box of laptops and files. "My protective instincts are in overdrive. I have this overwhelming urge to hover over Alex."

Mom smiled as she opened the front door and waved me through. "How's that working out for you?"

"So far, we're both trying to ignore it." I set the box on the table. "He flipped me off when I told him not to go out alone this morning, so it's just a matter of time before he gives me a smack-down."

"Then it's good you got away from him. He appreciates your protection, but it's more amusement than compliance. You need to do what you can to manage those instincts."

"I know that in my head, but my heart disagrees. I keep reminding myself that he's no longer that scared little kid who needs his big bad sister to make him feel safe."

Mom kissed my cheek. "I understand. My heart feels the same way about an angry little mage vampire girl."

"Yeah, but I'm a pain in the ass. Alex is sweet and kind."

"Until he isn't."

I nodded in agreement. "Until he isn't. Hey, Mom, what do you know about Roman?"

"He's not so bad as far as vampires go. I believe your dad is meeting with him now, as a matter of fact."

"Yeah. He approached me last night while I was pulling off my heist." I waved a hand toward the box. "He offered me a place in his house. When

I refused, we made a territory agreement that included him becoming part of the hybrid community and me being an honorary member."

I still wasn't sure how I felt about that. Between Roman, the purebloods after my brother, and good ole Jed showing up, my thoughts were jumbled. I had the urge to run away, which wasn't my style. I was more of a confront-your-problems-head-on kind of gal. That I had the urge to run pissed me off.

"Interesting." Mom hung her hat on a hook by the back door and ran magic over her hair to fix her hat head. "That should make your trips to Allure easier. But be careful with him. He's more agreeable than most vampires but still a powerful ancient."

I took the soda she offered and sat at the table. "We're blood-related. I'm always wary of blood relations." If there was one thing I'd learned by studying my vampire family, it was they were brutal and manipulative. I wouldn't be surprised if Roman gave me a false sense of security before he struck.

"Good. Roman says he rarely talks to your biological family. But vampires stick together, so try not to get too close until you can get a feel for the situation." She tapped her chin. "I'm still on the fence about your mage family."

I took a sip of soda. "Yeah. It might be too late for that warning." I slid the crumpled envelope out of my jacket and handed it to her. "Jed came by this morning and left that."

Her face paled. "This is Ara's writing."

"That's what I thought. Which means she knows about me."

"I bet she's leaving it up to Jedediah to bring you in."

"That explains a lot." If he were under pressure from his mother, the Queen of Vampires, then he'd do anything to bring me in. Tears sprung to my eyes, and I blinked them back. "I'm terrified, Mom. More scared than I've been in years. I don't know what to do."

She came around the table and wrapped me in a warm hug. "I'm so sorry, Firefly."

The tears I'd been holding back streamed down my cheeks. "I know."

She released me and handed me a tissue. "We always knew this would happen one day."

"Yep." I mopped up my tears. "What does she want with me?" And what would she do when she found me? I didn't know, but I bet it wouldn't be good.

Mom shook her head. "I don't know. I haven't been part of that community for years. But I doubt she would go to all the trouble of inviting you to dinner to harm you."

"You don't know that."

She leaned forward. "No. But I do know that you're *our* daughter, and we will not allow her to hurt you. Besides, Ara doesn't have the same brutal reputation as Jedediah. The vampires she takes in never want to leave her house. Maybe she'll surprise you."

"What if you're wrong?"

"Then I'll tell the Queen of Ahl about you. She's young and softhearted. There's no way she'd allow anything to happen to you when she finds out who you are."

I sniffed. "I doubt she'll care."

"We'll see. She's much stronger and smarter than people give her credit for and will be a great queen if given the chance."

"That's not what I heard." I'd heard rumors that her only concern was herself.

She smirked. "I've been snooping around your family and don't think it'll be as bad as you imagined. You can't hide from them forever, though I hoped we could ease you into meeting them. If you want, I'll go with you to that dinner."

A ton of weight lifted off my shoulders. I trusted my mom. If she said I'd be okay, then she'd make sure it happened. "Okay. I'll think it through and let you know."

"Good. Ara isn't so bad but steer clear of Jedediah. It's never pleasant when that vampire gets up to something."

"Your protective instincts kicking in?"

"Yes."

Dad strolled into the kitchen, sniffed the air, and eyed the tissue in my hand. "Why are you crying?"

"*Jedediah.*" Mom's tone made his name sound like a curse word. "He showed up at Lily's place this morning and dropped this off." She thrust the invitation at him.

Dad growled as he read it. The deep rumble made the house shake. "Did you talk to him?"

I rubbed my sensitive ears. "No. Alex told him to leave through the monitoring spell. He assumed Alex was my servant."

"Listen carefully and heed my advice. Stop all engagement with him and his spies. Do not beat them up, play games with them, or kill them. Jedediah is not a vampire you want to play with. He is ruthless and will stop at nothing to get what he wants. You and Alex need to consider moving back home, where we can better shield you from him."

The concern in his eyes caused my heart to make a little squishy flip. "I appreciate the offer. I really do. But moving back here would be a disaster for this family. You and I would be at each other's throats, and Alex would self-isolate to get away from all the babying." I waved a hand toward the battered invitation. "Mom thinks I need to attend that dinner."

He ran a hand through his hair. "I suppose you do. But I don't like it. If that woman so much as looks at you the wrong way, I'll kill her."

I shivered. He meant it. I was a little bit of a daddy's girl. "The purebloods are going to become a bigger problem soon."

"Agreed. Which means you and Alex aren't safe here," Mom said.

"We're fine."

Amber rolled across Dad's eyes. "You're not fine, so don't lie. You have two powerful vampires pursuing you, the Vampire Queen knows of your existence, and a powerful group is after Alex. You're in over your head. Don't play games and watch your ass."

I'd only ever seen my dad act like that once. To this day, I'm not sure he didn't kill my brother's biological family when they dumped him on us. I cleared my throat. "Why does this worry you so much?"

My parents shared a look. "Because the group amassing in town has planned for centuries to take over paranormals and lead us down a path of destruction. They've already caused quite a bit of trouble in the pockets."

The information I stole alluded to that, but I didn't know they'd already started to try to overthrow the crown. "The Sentinels?"

"Correct, though they used to be called the Bellicose."

I swallowed. "And they want Alex to join them."

"Correct."

My eyes slid to the box I brought. "They also want to enslave hybrids."

Dad roared.

I fought not to pee my pants. I'd never heard him roar like that outside of a fight.

He turned his glowing amber eyes to me and leaned in. "Remove. Yourself. From. The. Situation."

I held up my hand in the stop gesture. "Okay. I'm going to spy with Roman tonight, and after that, consider me removed. But if they attack Alex, all bets are off."

"Follow Roman's lead, then stay behind your wards. If you're attacked, lead them to us, and we'll fight them here. If you find yourself boxed in, head to Allure and get a hotel," Mom said in a calm, even voice. She rested her hand on Dad's, completely unaffected by his roar. "I've arranged for protection while you're there."

"Not a chance in hell I'll seek refuge with the purebloods."

"Watch your language. And you will if you want to save your brother."

"You just had to play the protection card," I joked, trying to lighten the atmosphere. It didn't work. "Fine. But only if there's no other option."

"No. You'll go there before they attack you in front of humans and expose us. I'll not have you blamed for the inevitable."

"Fine."

Mom leaned in, her blue eyes serious. "Promise me, Lily."

As I headed home, I played the exchange with them over and over in my head. Dad had to be super worried to lose control like that. Or under a lot of pressure. I knew he'd never hurt me, but his anger still made me nervous. If we were to go to Allure, my biological family would find me. But if we stayed, we'd have to cower behind our wards. I didn't like either option.

When I got home, I peered out the back door to see Alex on the porch with his laptop. Cavil sat across from him, the two in a serious conversation, probably working on building a god-sized financial empire. I needed sleep before we went out to spy. I hoped Roman could help me learn more about the pureblood group and maybe shed some light on my grandmother's motivations before that dinner.

Before heading to my room, I gave Alex and Cavil one last look.

Our house was custom-built and too big for the two of us. The main living area was an open concept, with two offices on one side and two bedrooms and a shared bathroom on the other. The second floor was split into separate areas. Alex's private domain was on the left, while mine was on the right. Each had three bedrooms and two bathrooms. Having our own space curbed our territorial instincts. I originally bought the land intending to live alone, but Alex insisted on moving in with me, claiming I needed someone to watch my back. He was one of the few people I could stand in large doses, so I agreed. The separate private areas were my idea.

I went to the far end of the hall to my bedroom, closed the door, and fell face-first on the bed.

Chapter Eight

"Move quieter and always keep your ears open." Roman's voice was barely audible, even to my sensitive ears, as we crept across the roof of a restaurant. "You are a powerful vampire for your age, so this should come easy to you. Once you practice enough, it will become second nature."

Roman's teachings were as dull as they were long-winded, but I still appreciated the guidance. I couldn't convince him I was a born vampire, so he kept trying to get me to do things like a newbie. He thought I was powerful for my age because Jed turned me. Once I realized I'd never convince him, I gave it up and started soaking up his boring lessons. They were much too basic for my skill level.

Rubbing my nose to erase the fried food scent, I brought my strange mix of mage and vampire magic to the surface and continued to scamper across the rooftop. "Where are we going?"

He ducked behind an air conditioner. "Just there." He pointed to a warehouse a few blocks away.

"Then why are we walking across roofs and whispering?"

"For practice, of course. Now, try to blend into this shadow." He pointed at the air conditioner.

I slid into the shadows and wrapped them around me, the only way I'd ever done it. Then sank back further when a look of disgust settled on his face.

Roman's hand shot out and grabbed my shoulder. "No, no, Lily. You're doing it all wrong. It is a mistake many young vampires make, so don't fret. We will take action to correct that issue, and you will soon be a pro. Now, instead of wrapping the shadow around you, you must connect your magic to it."

I let out a breath. "I dunno, Uncle Roman. My magic does weird stuff like attract the human crazies." He'd insisted I call him Uncle Roman or Uncle when we'd met up for our little excursion. It made me uncomfortable because handing out family titles all willy-nilly didn't come naturally to me. They were something people had to earn. I made an exception for Roman so I could keep the peace and get some vampire training.

"It attracts meals, not crazies. As you so graciously pointed out yesterday, vampires are forbidden from preying on the good humans. When we use too much magic, it calls acceptable meals to us. You will find more turn up in the human world than in the pockets because they have no resistance to our magic."

"Oh." I took a second to think about that because it didn't sound right to me. "I don't have a problem when I shadow blend or go fluid. Only when I try to use my mage magic."

Roman tapped his chin. "The First, Jonas, told me that your magics have blended into the most unique power. Perhaps use less when doing your spells, and you won't have the side effects." He shook his head. "I am uncertain that is the answer because I've never met a successfully turned mage who didn't go insane from the virus. To better blend in, you must merge with the shadow. Don't force it, and let it come naturally. It is in your nature, so it is a basic skill. Go ahead and give it a try."

"You might want to stand back," I mumbled as I sunk into the shadows. Magic gushed through me like a raging river when I pulled it forward. Heart pounding, I wrestled with it by imagining a dam until the flow slowed. The amount of power that wanted to escape meant I needed to go to Allure and let some out soon, or it would explode. I let one drop through and touched the shadow with it.

Boom!

Roman and I tumbled in different directions. Pieces of air conditioner bit into me like razor-sharp blades as they stabbed through my clothes. I stretched out a hand, latched onto the rain gutter on the back of the building to slow myself, then let go and landed on the ground in a crouch. "Ow."

I'd pulled half the chunks of metal out of myself when Roman appeared. He pulled a piece of fan out of his leg as he watched me. His brow creased. "You heal fast for your age."

"Yes. My mom says my mage side makes my healing abilities unique." The vampire virus allowed even new vampires to heal fast. As they aged, they healed faster. Because of my mage heritage, I got a double-dose of healing, so mine was as fast as Roman's.

"Interesting." He glanced at the roof of the building. "That was most unexpected."

"Not really." He had far fewer metal shards sticking out of him than me. I pulled the last few out as sirens sounded in the distance. "Let's get out of here."

We went fluid and stopped a block away from the target warehouse. Roman plucked a chunk of metal out of his arm. "You have the power of a much older vampire. Yet you are only a few years out of transition. I wonder if turning a mage is wise."

"Except I'm not turned. I was born this way."

"Yes, yes. I know you think that, but I highly doubt it."

"Why?"

"Because the only way you could be a born vampire is if the Vampire Queen had a third child. Which is impossible due to a mishap when she was younger. She enjoys watching her two children struggle to prove themselves worthy." He waved a hand. "You are a true gem, and I will take great pride in being your ally and watching you grow."

I frowned. The guy made a convincing case. I wouldn't put it past the two idiots who birthed me to change a baby mage. "How do you know that?"

"Although I have not spoken about it to her in many years, I doubt my sister has changed her mind about a third child. It would be much easier if you would meet her. She is quite skilled in reading these things." He waved a hand as if dismissing the thought. "I know that is not ideal. Do not use your shadow skills tonight. Stick close to me, and I will hide you if needed."

I stayed close to Roman and watched how he hid us in the shadows on a roof across from a busy warehouse. It seemed more like he connected his vampire essence rather than magic. I could have facepalmed when I realized that was what he meant. He didn't have mage magic, so why would I ever think connecting to shadows meant using mine? Stupid.

We watched as carloads of purebloods lined the otherwise empty streets. We'd already knocked out the guards on the roof, and Roman took their human-style radios so we could listen to the chatter. Every once in a while, he'd check in using a voice close to one of the unconscious guys.

"They're all men." Paranormals didn't have a patriarchy like humans. They practiced classism based on magical power but not sexism. It was rare to see a crowd of purebloods of only one gender.

"Yes. It is most unusual," Roman said in the same low tone.

A five-car motorcade rounded the corner and stopped in the center of the silent crowd. The radio squawked. "Commander one in the third car. Stay alert."

"Ten-four," came multiple responses.

Several mid-level mages, witches, and shifters poured out of the cars and lined up on each side of the walkway as if forming a reception line. The back door of the third car swung open, and a tall, dark-haired man stepped out and straightened his jacket.

The crowd cheered.

He offered them a half-hearted wave, then projected his voice. "Silence!"

The sound cut off.

"We are on the path to victory. We will destroy the palace and defeat the fake queen!"

The crowd didn't make a sound.

"You may applaud."

They did, but with way too much enthusiasm.

Heart in my throat, I slid further into the shadows.

The man's head turned toward us, his eyes glowing with a kind of sickly brown glow. He smirked, revealing sharp yellow teeth, then leaned over and whispered something to a guy on the sidewalk. That guy disappeared into the building.

"We must take our leave." Roman latched onto my arm and went fluid. We shimmied down the side of the building.

"We've got them." The shout came from our right.

I whipped around. At least twenty shifters, mages, and witches surrounded us. All low or mid-level. A giant stood at the back of the crowd. My fangs extended. "You take left. I'll take right."

"Very well." Roman sent out a burst of power as six-inch claws formed on his hands and feet. He dove for the closest shifter and slashed his other hand across the one on the left. The one on the right dropped to the ground, his throat torn out.

I shook my head, extended my own claws, and dove into the crowd.

A witch tried to spell me, so I stabbed him in the heart before kicking another witch's knees, shattering them. There weren't too many opportunities to use my full strength, and I reveled in it.

I kicked someone's head with the claws on my feet, then swung my elbow back and smashed a guy in the face. Then went fluid and zipped around in circles, kicking, punching, and clawing. I flipped, landed on the back of one, and did a jumping-jack for good measure, breaking his spine. Launching myself at the giant, I latched on to his throat with my fangs so fast he didn't see me coming. I stabbed my claws into his chest and dislodged myself without unlatching my fangs.

Two wolves raced toward me from each side. I waited until the last second and moved out of the way. They smashed into each other at full speed. I threw my arm around the neck of one and twisted, then kicked the other one in the head with the claws on my feet before they recovered from the collision.

When I looked for my next victim, there were none.

The street was too quiet.

I cocked my head and listened.

Fabric rustled to my right, and I spun in that direction.

That's when I realized three additional vampires stood across the street, two with open mouths and wide eyes. Roman had resumed his human form. He stood next to Jed's goon and two other vampires, arms crossed and eyebrows pinched together.

I retracted my claws and fangs. "What?"

Roman waved a hand. "We shall discuss it later, niece. Right now, we must retreat."

I pointed at the other vampires. "Who are they?"

"My house members, of course."

I moved my finger toward Jed's spy. "And him?"

His bloody grin made my skin crawl. "Edmund is mine now."

Noise from down the road pulled me out of my shock. We went fluid and headed to where I parked. I pulled a couple of sheets of plastic from the back and handed one to Edmund and one to the guy who'd thrown me out on my ass when I went to Roman for help. "Cover the seats and carpet. I don't want blood all over my van."

When he complied without comment, I pushed the button to shut the back, then turned to Roman and raised an eyebrow. "Why is Edmund here?"

Roman grinned. "I couldn't allow a vampire to harass people in my territory, so I gave him the choice of either death or relocation. He chose wisely."

I blinked. "Cool. But how are you going to keep the weasel from reporting to Jed?"

His smile revealed blood-soaked teeth. "I have a difficult time remembering how ignorant you are. I am older and more powerful than Jedediah. Therefore, my blood bond circumvents his. I ordered Edmund to silence, and he had no choice but to comply. You see, age trumps ego and birthright within the vampire hierarchy, except perhaps in your case. You seem more powerful than most, and I'm excited to work with you to figure out why."

I held up a hand to stop his speech. I didn't want to be there all night listening to him ramble. "That's genius. Can you do that for everyone Jed sends?"

"I will need a full house if I plan to protect..." He hesitated. "My territory and the hybrids within it. The First Jonas negotiated that little nugget. Any uninvited vampire who comes to the city will either join a house or die."

So yes. Roman was nice for a vampire, but still cunning and lethal. I needed to remember that. And stay on his good side. I decided calling him uncle wasn't such a big concession. Besides, the more people willing to protect Alex, the better. "There's been a lot of vampires lurking around the city. You can't possibly take them all."

"Oh, yes, I have noticed that. The Queen of Ahl requested their presence. She is the foremost authority, you see. Even when you live in the human world. Jedediah's vampires are not invited and, therefore, are available for the taking. It is merely a matter of semantics. One must be mindful while building a house, so not all vampires will qualify."

I blinked. "Okay." I didn't know the queen cared enough to help us, though I should have since Mom met with her.

Edmund finished applying the plastic and bowed to me. "Your car is now protected, Mistress. Do you need me to do anything else?"

"I'm not your mistress, so don't call me that. Let's get out of here." I hopped into the driver's side before Roman could correct me with another long-winded speech.

CHAPTER NINE

WHEN WE FILED INTO the kitchen, Alex froze with a bite of cereal halfway to his mouth. It wasn't every day a parade of half-naked vampires walked through your mudroom. We'd stripped our clothes off in the garage so we didn't track blood through the house. I handed out sweats we kept in a spare bedroom for our rescues, pointed out the two guest bathrooms, and headed to my room to clean up.

After I showered and changed, I joined them downstairs. The three vampires sat in the breakfast nook, sipping water. Alex swept his mop of brown hair out of his face. "Um, Lily, why did you bring Jed's spies home?"

"Edmund is no longer Jed's spy." I pointed at Roman, who emerged clean and wearing a pair of red sweats. "Alex, meet Roman, the local House Master. He's older and more powerful than Jed and able to steal his vampires."

Alex's mouth fell open. "And he finds it fun." He tapped his temple. "You might want to guard your thoughts around me. They seep through."

Roman smiled, his teeth no longer bloody. "Oh, my, another absolute treasure. Ann Marie was always good at finding unique things. However, most people give credit to Jonas since he's a First. Very nice to meet you, young Alex."

Alex blinked. "Sure. What happened to your clothes?"

We took turns explaining what happened.

When we finished, Alex burst into laughter.

"What is so funny?" Roman asked.

He wiped his eyes. "Sorry. You really think Lily was turned as a baby?"

Roman nodded. "It's more likely than her being a natural-born vampire. Only the Queen of Umbra can give birth to vampires, and Lily claims her mother is a mage. However, I do not doubt she is a blood relation, probably from a human descendant. I had three human children before Lilith took away that privilege, you see. From them, I have many descendants. My sister, on the other hand, was gifted with the ability to birth vampires rather than humans. Jedediah may have found one of my descendants or a mage with a drop of our blood and turned her."

Umbra was the original name of vampires. When the humans started calling us vampires, it caught on, but the queen kept the title Queen of Umbra. I shifted in my seat. The conversation made me uncomfortable.

Alex ignored me. "And how do you explain her weirdness?"

"I'm sorry, but I do not understand."

"Lily has four sets of claws and four fangs when other vampires have two. She's almost as powerful as you. Yet, you're older than dirt while she's young. Turned vampires can't keep up with her, so I don't think your theory is right."

"Ah, yes. Perhaps because she is a mage who was turned very young. I have seen the impact of that before, you see. Though it has been many years. Mages whom vampires attempted to turn either died or became addled. So the Firsts Lilith and Lissa found a way to make other magical beings immune to vampirism, but there might be exceptions. Like turning a baby mage before she's gifted with magic."

My stomach sank. Cavil told me I wasn't a mage or a vampire, so maybe what Roman said was true. If so, then who the hell was I? What if my bitch of a mother hired Jed to turn a baby? I rubbed my temples. No, because then I'd need a House Master and to drink blood. Unless she also used some kind of weird magic to ensure I didn't. My mother was so sure I'd become what she wanted me to be when I was a kid that his story didn't make sense.

I remembered the moment she realized that wouldn't happen. She'd trapped a woodland sprite in a metal cage and brought me in to torture it for information. I refused. She tried to make me, but I'd grown more powerful than her. I was a kid, but I'd never forget the combination of rage and disappointment on her face when she realized she'd never control me. Not long after that incident, she dumped me at Jed's house.

I cried for two days after he threw me in that shack. Then, spent a lot of time wondering if I should have tortured the poor sprite. The sadness turned to burning anger, and I spent the rest of my stay using it as fuel. The rage helped me decide I would never be like her, nor would I live under Jed's thumb. I paid attention to other vampires and noticed how different I was from them. As soon as I broke free, I studied everything I could find written about my biological parents, their abilities, and their reputations. I asked my adoptive parents every question I could think of. And vowed to never become an asshole like them.

If Roman was right, then the identity I created was a lie. A lot of my self-image revolved around being a natural-born vampire. If I wasn't, where did that leave me? I swallowed back the tears that wanted to fall. "It doesn't matter. Come on, guys. I'll drive you home."

Alex insisted on going with us. He sat in the middle seat with the guy who turned me away at Roman's house. Twice. I made Edmund and a vampire whose name I didn't bother to learn sit in the third seat.

We'd only gone a couple of miles when I noticed a line of cars approaching from behind. Although not uncommon during the day, it was the middle of the night. "We have company. Let Dad know we're coming in hot." I turned left toward our parent's house instead of right toward the freeway and stepped on it. We still had seven miles to their house, and although my minivan was kickass, it wasn't made for speed.

They were gaining on us.

Alex waved his phone. "He wants to know how many."

"Edmund, try to get a count. Guy who rejected me...sorry, I never got your name. Help Edmund."

"His name is Folami," Roman answered. "He is my oldest friend and my most trusted house member. You will find holding onto vampires you trust is wise. It is much like how you cling to your adopted family. However, the blood bond makes you much closer. If you agreed to join my house, you could experience this first-hand."

The long-winded lesson at an inappropriate time did not surprise me, nor did the dig about joining his house. "Right." The tires screeched when I took a corner too fast. "Two miles out, coming in from the south."

"Yeah, I got that since they're my parents, too, and I know where they live. Hey Lily, are we there yet? Are we there yet? Are we there yet?"

"Ha ha."

"I count fifteen cars, different sizes and shapes. If we figure five people per car, that's at least seventy-five adversaries." Folami's voice had a deep, smooth timber to it.

"Wow. I bet you have no problem talking the ladies into giving you a little snack with that voice."

I glanced in the mirror in time to see a small smile. "Thank you, Mistress. We all have our talents. Mine is voice persuasion."

"That's handy. We can use that. Team up with my mom. She's a sorceress who can amplify your voice."

"Dad says to go to field three." Alex slipped his phone in his jacket and zipped it.

"I do not think we should split into teams. I understand the First Jonas and his match are very powerful, but we are greatly outnumbered," Roman said.

Alex snorted. "You've never seen our family fight together."

After I took a right onto a dirt road that led to a field at the edge of the property, I slowed. I wasn't sure who was right. Our family was a force, but we'd never fought that many people before, and if the powerful demon was with them, we might be screwed. I parked behind the barn and hopped out. "Alex, we're going to have to carry you."

"Nope." He shifted, shook his enormous body, and swung his massive square head toward me. Alex was so big in his shifted form that his face was level with mine. His ancient bloodline made him much larger than modern-day lions. He roared.

It rattled my bones and blew out my sensitive ears. I rubbed them as I fought the urge to run. Two of Roman's vampires bolted toward the shadows. "Cute."

He took off in a beige blur. The kid was fast for an eight-hundred-pound lion, but not as fast as a vampire.

"That's a big cat. What is he?"

"No time, Roman. Let's go." I went fluid, confident the other vampires would follow.

We caught up to Alex in a heartbeat and let him set the pace.

When we were kids, we played with those roadside speed-check stations. Alex's top speed was fifty miles per hour. While I could go so fast, my speed didn't register. Letting Alex set the pace meant that I had to intermittently go fluid and run while the other vampires kept a steady pace. I hoped Roman could teach me how to do that.

Our parents stood in the center of the field. Mom's flowing yellow sundress fluttered in the wind. Dad was nude. Living with two shifters, I was used to the nudity, so it didn't bother me. As a group, we stopped in front of them.

"Report," Dad ordered.

The vampires, including Roman, took a step back.

I gave them a short version of the story. When I was done, his eyes glowed. "And why didn't you tell me all of this?"

"The demon and the other fight just happened a couple of hours ago."

He ran a hand through his hair and tilted his head toward the road, where our pursuers stopped. "You need to stop playing spy before you stir up more shit than you can flush."

"That doesn't even make sense."

"You know what I mean." He grunted before turning his attention to Roman. "You take the right side where they're trying to flank us. The wards are down in this field, and only this field, so don't stray. Holler if you need backup." He pointed to Folami. "You take the left. Use your voice as a weapon on as many as possible. Alex, you're with your mom. Try to pluck as much information from their heads as you can. Lily, with me. No one moves until I shift. Fight to kill."

We crouched in the field and watched as the bad guys maneuvered into position. They were mostly shifters, but I spotted an ogre, a few low to mid-level witches, and two mages. Three demons led them. Their movements were jerky and uneven. I sensed a fraction of the power compared to the one at the warehouse. Not a single one noticed Alex creeping toward them in the tall grass. The demon in the middle stepped forward. Its eyes ran over me before settling on dad. "Hand over the mental mage, and we will give you a favorable position amongst the slaves."

"What an honor," I mumbled.

Dad rested his hand on my shoulder. "Leave the city now or die."

The demon snickered. "Shifters are always so bold. At first. You will hand over the mental mage, or we will kill you and rape your women."

My dad had the patience of a saint. Not much ever got under his skin. The one exception was when someone threatened people he loved, especially Mom.

He shifted so fast I had to go fluid to keep from getting crushed.

The demon's eyes widened when Dad opened his long, crocodile-like snout. I jammed my fingers in my ears before he roared.

The ground shook as he charged.

I swallowed and tried to ignore the blind panic that came with the sound. Something I wouldn't be able to do if I hadn't had years of practice. Then I went fluid and hopped on his giant clawed foot behind a lump.

Dad stomped on the demon with his other foot and ground him into the dirt.

I tightened my grip when he charged and waited for him to slow down. When he did, I hopped off and sprinted toward the witches.

He crushed them before I got there and let out another roar.

I threw my hand in the air. "Spinosaurus for the win!"

He kicked his leg out and flicked a toe. It launched me into the air toward a group of mages throwing spells at Mom. My claws and fangs were out, and I gutted them before they knew I was there. Alex flew by, smashed into the chest of a mountain lion shifter, and ripped out his throat. He gave me a cat-grin as the group trying to surround us fell to the ground. He must have crushed their brains with his mental magic.

"Show off!" I shouted as I went fluid, stabbing and kicking anything in my path as I made a loop to get behind Mom.

As soon as we were clear, she threw up her arms. White light streamed through the field, reducing a group of shifters to ash.

I blinked until some of my vision returned. It was dumb to watch Mom's magic while in a fight. As soon as I could see again, I raced under Dad's tail and scattered a group of witches who were dumb enough to throw spells at Roman.

"He's a vampire, you idiots!" I crashed into them, kicked one in the groin, and stabbed another in the neck. One threw an acidic spell at me. It rolled off and sizzled on the ground. "And so am I." I kicked him in the stomach, curled my toe-claws for maximum damage, then moved on.

Roman ripped out the throat of the last one.

Dad used his nimble tail to crush a group of shifters and ran after the ogre, who kept trying to smash Alex over the head with his fist. Alex toyed with the guy until he felt Dad's seventy-ton body shake the ground as he ran. Then he bolted in my direction.

The ogre tried to run but didn't make it far before an enormous foot landed on him. I smirked as I turned to see who to attack next, but the field was quiet.

Mom used magic to pile their bodies in a field and called a local phoenix family to come burn them.

"Do you see this, Lily?" She stood with her hands on her hips.

There wasn't anything to see, so I turned on my magic sight. And gasped. "What is that stuff?"

"It's the magic they're using to control people. Vampires aren't immune." She ran a burst of white magic over Roman and his people.

"Thank you. It is very kind of you to look after us." He turned his attention to me. "We must be going, Lily. We will find our way home."

They disappeared.

Mom shoved a vial into my hand. "Take that. It will make you immune to that magic."

I swigged it and felt a tingle of clean magic wash over me. "How did you get it to work on vampires?"

"I didn't. A witch who works with the Queen of Ahl figured it out. I expanded on her idea."

"Neat," I said as I watched Alex swig his.

It was always fun to watch a phoenix work. Their fire was so hot there wasn't much smoke. When they were done, Mom used a spell to bury the evidence, and the four of us trudged toward my van.

Dad stared at the ground in deep thought as we walked. As we neared the road, his head swung toward me. "You and Alex need to stick together. Let Roman and his crew spy until they quit targeting you."

"They're not after Lily. They're after me," Alex said. "Lily's trying to get them to target her, but they see her as an obstacle. They think we're matched, so they want her dead."

"Now, that's just insulting."

Mom shoulder-checked me. "It's not a challenge, so don't treat it as one."

I shrugged. "I agree with Dad. Alex shouldn't be alone, and other than you guys, I'm the best person to watch his back. If I remember right, I've already agreed to remove myself from the situation. I'm happy to let Roman spy because he's way better than I am. Besides, his vampire lessons are so long-winded I'd rather stay ignorant." I didn't mention he almost convinced me that I was a turned vampire. My parents didn't need to know how much that bothered me.

"Good," Dad said as we reached the van.

I held up a finger. "I promised Cavil I'd go to Allure with him to look for houses. Thanks to you guys, he seems to be on a lightning-fast path toward world domination."

Dad threw his head back and laughed. "As far as gods go, Cavil isn't even in the top five for showing up and wrapping the world around his finger. He's one of the good ones, I think. We'll help him where we can. He makes for a powerful ally."

Mom eyed the road. "You always find the most interesting rescues, Lily. When are you going?"

"As soon as he auctions off some artifacts, I guess. You think he's really a god?"

"He has the same magic signature and goals as other gods, so I'm going to say yes."

Alex's mouth hung open. "You talk about them like one showing up here is a regular thing. Just how many gods are there?"

"I've been away from the magical community for too long, so I don't know exactly. But I can guarantee there's at least a couple."

I handed a fresh plastic paint cover to Alex. "It doesn't matter. Like you two always say, we set people up for success, and we don't discriminate. Cavil deserves a chance just like everyone else."

The next afternoon, Alex and I drove around the areas where we'd spotted the purebloods to see if they operated during the day. We took Alex's SUV because they knew my van.

Alex pulled into the parking lot of Hooves and turned off the engine. "Let's hope Dale heard something. This is boring, and I have work to do."

I sighed. "Your right. It's one of the dumbest ideas I've ever had. If he doesn't know anything, we can go home."

Dale's eyes narrowed when he spotted us. He poured us sparkling water as we slid onto stools in the center of the bar.

"Guess we're drinking water today," I mumbled.

His lips twitched. "What brings you two here so early?"

Alex pushed his glasses up his nose. "Hey, Dale. We wondered if you've seen more of those purebloods."

"Why?"

"We had to kill a bunch of them last night."

"No shit? Why didn't you call? I would have loved to help with that."

Alex shrugged. "It was at our parents' house."

"Ahhh. I see. What did they do to draw the ire of our local First?"

I took a sip of the unwanted water. "Those guys have their hearts set on Alex joining their gang. We took offense to that."

"As one does." Dale rubbed his chin. "We have a couple here every night. More on the weekends. It's screwing with our business because hybrids want nothing to do with those f...guys. What can we do to help?"

"I don't think there's much you *can* do other than get information."

"Speaking of information, do you know where they're staying?" Alex asked.

Dale shook his head. "I heard a couple of rumors, but I'm not sure how accurate they are."

I nodded. "We'll be glad to check them out."

"I heard they've been buying apartment complexes around town, including the one on the edge of this neighborhood. The hybrids nearby are ready to sell their houses and move west."

"Interesting." I set my glass down. "Why haven't we heard any of this?"

"You know how Sheila is. She wants to pretend we don't need the First. Ann Marie has known for weeks, from what I've gathered. Rumor has it she's working with the Queen herself."

Sheila was the hybrid leader responsible for West Boise. The woman had a bit of an ego. And Mom would do what she needed to do to protect the hybrids. She even circumvented my insane biological mother once. Which was not something many people accomplished.

Alex nodded. "So, Sheila convinced people she'd handle it to settle them down but doesn't have a clue what to do? That's just dumb."

Dale's intense gaze focused on my brother. "Stay out of my head, kid."

"Sorry. It just happens sometimes." He threw money on the bar. "Lily and I will check it out."

I slid off the bar stool. "Keep your head down, Dale. Those guys are bad news."

"Explain."

"A powerful demon leads the group. We think they have mind-control magic and want to enslave hybrids. Go see Mom when you can. She has an immunity potion."

Alex nodded. "They also have a lot of loyal followers. Be careful with them and text our dad if anything goes down."

Dale inclined his head. "We'll head their way in the morning. Keep me posted."

"Do you think it was a good idea to warn him?" Alex asked as we made our way through the subdivision.

"He would have figured it out eventually. Bartenders hear everything. I wouldn't be surprised if that's why they opened a bar in the first place."

The large apartment complex popped up in the last couple of years. It wasn't unusual for the area, but it made it easy for the purebloods to slide in without humans noticing. As far as evil plans went, it wasn't bad.

I craned my neck to get a better look when we drew near. My stomach sank when nothing unusual stood out. I didn't know what I was expecting. It's not like they'd post a sign outside that said, 'bad guys live here.'

Alex pulled into a convenience store down the street and stopped beside a gas pump. "Let's go home, Lily. We're not going to solve this today."

"Sure." I turned on my rarely used magic sight as I waited for him. It was risky, but the sight used such a tiny amount of power I doubted it would draw too many crazies. And we'd be long gone before they gravitated toward me. Black magic swirled around the entire complex in swaths. "Alex, turn on your sight."

His mouth fell open. "What the hell is that stuff?"

I pulled out my phone and sent a quick text to Mom. "It's that same magic as the guys from last night."

"We're immune now, right?" Alex pointed to the neighborhood behind the apartments. "Let's park there and walk closer."

We stopped across the street from the apartment complex. I leaned forward and examined the magic. It wiggled. The stuff looked like a bug infestation. My stomach rolled as I brushed off my arms and scratched my head. "Gross."

"You're so embarrassing." Alex tilted his head and sniffed the air. "It smells diseased. I noticed it last night, but it wasn't this bad."

"Yes, it does. And the sight of bugs makes me itch." I scratched my knee.

"It's not even touching you. Don't be such a baby."

"I'm going to need another shower."

"You've had enough showers for three people the last few days."

I scratched my back. "True."

Alex grabbed my arm and pulled me away from the writhing black goo magic. "Come on. Let's get out of here before you open a gaping wound in your arm."

I took one last look, then released my magic sight. I scratched my stomach, then my cheek. "That's so gross. It's like they thought, 'hey, what's the best way to give people the heebie-jeebies? Oh, wait, bugs. Bugs are awesome.' Then they rubbed their hands together like a bunch of evil movie villains."

"I'm just glad to find something that really freaks you out. I wish I knew that when I was a kid. It would have been fun to leave bugs everywhere and watch you squirm."

I scratched my head, then brushed off my shoulders. "Mom would have killed you if you brought a single bug into her house."

"Sure, but it would have been worth it." His face grew serious. "What feelings did you get from that stuff?"

"Besides itchy, it felt like it was both calling to and repelling me. Kind of like...it wanted to test me for something. What did you get?"

"A solid invitation. I think they might use that magic to recruit, maybe even to control people. We should take Dad's advice and stay home. I want nothing to do with that stuff."

Chapter Ten

We stayed home for days. Alex had no problem with that because he had a job. I, on the other hand, wasn't much of a homebody. Nor did I need to sleep every day. So, I spent my days arguing with my foul-mouthed gnome and nights going fluid around the property to release some energy.

I was on my fourth lap when the familial tingle stabbed through my chest, followed by the wards pinging. Roman said he'd stop by with an update, so I headed toward the gates without thinking. Jed stood just beyond them. I froze. Dumb of me not to pay better attention to the level of tingling.

His eyes swept over me, and anger flashed through them before his face formed the fakest smile I'd ever seen. "Hello, Liliana. You're looking well."

"Leave." I couldn't keep the wobble out of my voice.

He fake-chuckled. "It hurts that you fear me. I only want to visit my daughter."

"I'm not your daughter."

A fake sigh. "Playing dumb is inappropriate for a vampire of your caliber, Liliana. I know you can feel the family ties." He slipped a letter through the gate and then dropped it when I didn't reach out. "That will help you understand your circumstances better."

My shoulders relaxed a little when Alex stepped out of the house and started toward me.

I almost jumped out of my skin when Roman appeared in front of him and folded his arms. "Jedediah. I do not recall you informing me you'd be visiting someone in my territory. Now, as you know, that is against the rules. I see you've brought many vampires with you. It just so happens I'm building my house, so I will take some off your hands for the indiscretion."

Jed took a small step back. "Hello, Roman. I should have known you were active when a member of my house disappeared."

"Oh, yes. Your vampire repeatedly breached my territory without permission and harassed one of my strongest allies." He extended his arm to its full length and awkwardly patted Jed on the shoulder. "I had no other choice but to act, lest I seem weak. After all, what kind of housemaster would I be to let something like that slide?" He eyed the four vampires behind Jed.

The slimeball's entire demeanor shifted from hostile to congenial. "I request a boon because I was not informed your house is active." He waved a hand. "We will leave as soon as I speak to my daughter."

I pressed my lips together to keep from commenting. I hoped Roman didn't fall for his fake kindness.

"Oh, my. I fear there is a misunderstanding here. You see, you lost the privilege of calling yourself Lily's maker when you abused, abandoned, and attempted to kill her. Since she is in my territory and is not feral..." He shrugged. "I'm sure you understand."

"Did Roman just claim you?" Alex's question was barely audible, even to my vampire ears.

I folded my arms to hide the shaking. I didn't need my baby brother to see how scared I was. "No."

Roman held up a hand. "You misunderstand me, young Alex. I am Lily's ally, not her master. Unfortunately, her maker rejected her without proper training. It's a shame, really, considering her power. I have taken over vampire monitoring within the territory until she learns, which will not take long. As a valuable ally, Lily can do as she wishes without my permission, of course." He grinned and rubbed his hands together. "What a fortunate gift you gave me when you chose that path, Jedediah. She is a true gem."

Jed's face paled. "She is not a made vampire, Roman, and you know it. As my biological daughter, she belongs to me, no matter the circumstances."

I fought to keep my fangs from popping out. "What a crock of shit. The only relationship you ever established was calling me an abomination and sending your goons to rape and kill me."

Roman held up a finger. "He also killed all but one vampire in his house who was kind to you. We mustn't forget that."

Jed waved a well-manicured, arrogant hand. "There is no proof of that, so it didn't happen. Liliana is mine, and I will go to the queen if I must." He leaned forward. "And you know I'll win because I always do."

"Lie." Alex tapped his nose. "That's some stinky bullshit you just dumped. Or did you forget a shifter was close?"

"Interesting." Roman clapped his hands once. "Now, since these vampires failed to check in with me and helped you harass my ally, I will take them as my own."

Jed stomped toward the car. "You cannot take my security detail for such a minor infraction."

"I'm surprised you don't know the rules about territory breaches, Jedediah. Because I only recently became active, I will give you a break this time and take only one. Rest assured, if you don't report in next time, I shall take them all."

"Get in the car!" Jed's voice was laced with persuasion.

The vampires didn't move, and I wondered if they hated him or if Roman somehow held them in thrall. If so, I needed to learn that skill. "Young Alex, which one of these fine vampires is the best candidate for my house?"

"You will not take my vampires."

Alex slid his hands in his pockets. "The redhead. She hates her current situation and is looking for a change. She's also a fan of yours."

Roman swatted Jed away when he tried to block him. He grew one claw, slashed the woman's wrist, and took a taste of her blood. Then he did the same to his wrist and held it up to her as an offering. Her shoulders sagged in relief as she accepted.

I didn't know blood bonds were that simple. Not that I ever planned to create one.

Jed and the other three vampires piled into the car. The tires squealed as they sped away.

"Now, Lily. A vampire can only be stolen from a weaker housemaster. Should you decide to build a house, you will need guidance on how to add the proper amount of intention to form bonds. I, of course, will be glad to help. In addition, should Jedediah ever try to force one on you, you can refuse. They must be consensual, you see."

"Right." I eyed the newest member of Roman's house, who beamed at him like he was a rock star. "So, uh, would you like to come in?"

"Oh, I better not. I must get my new house member settled and integrated. I will have Edmund email you an update on our spying duties."

"Sure." I eyed his new vampire. "I'm Lily, by the way, and this is my brother, Alex."

Her attention snapped to me. "I'm Senga. Thanks for choosing me, Alex. I hated that house." Her voice had a touch of a Scottish accent.

Alex offered her a small smile. "No problem."

"Senga is also the oldest and most powerful of the four. She will make a fine addition. We shall get you settled." They disappeared.

Neither of us moved for a few seconds.

Alex pulled his hands out of his pockets. "Why do conversations with that man exhaust me?"

I snorted. "He's long-winded, for sure. I think it's part of his personality."

"Maybe. I hope he doesn't wear you down to the point you look at him with googly eyes like his new vampire did."

"You don't have to worry about that. Roman's nicer than other vampires, but he still raises the hairs on the back of my neck."

I waited until we were in the house to read the letter that Jed had dropped on the ground. It held a list of addresses of the invading purebloods, and he had more detailed information about them. Of course, he wouldn't give it to me unless I attended that dinner. I handed the letter to Alex.

He scanned the addresses and whistled. "Jed is as good as Roman at getting what he wants. Right now, he wants something from you. He's dangling bait like you're a dumb fish. The question is, are you going to bite?"

"No. I'm going to scan this and email it to Dad. They can check out those addresses to see if they're legit."

My phone pinged. I pulled it out and tried not to smile when I saw a text from Cavil. He wanted to know if I'd be available to go to Allure the next day. I texted the family group asking if Mom or Dad could stay with Alex.

He rolled his eyes as he read it. "Is this the part where I remind you I'm a grown man and don't need a babysitter? Because I am."

"You heard Dad. He doesn't want you to go anywhere alone."

"And you, who never met a rule she didn't break, will follow this one?"

"I follow the rules. Sometimes. Besides, those guys the other night were only a couple of miles from here. Chances are they're waiting for you to be alone to pounce."

"They'll never get in here."

My phone buzzed with a text from Mom saying she'd stay with him. I smirked. "Too late now."

I slept like the dead that night. Pun intended. I was bored and wanted to be at full strength when I released some magic and dealt with Cavil. Maybe being well-rested would help me circumvent his contracts. Although, other than vowing his life to me, none of them were that serious.

I sipped from my second cup of coffee when the wards alerted me that someone had breached them. By the time I made it to the front of the house, two cars were already halfway down the driveway. Mom parked in front of the garage. A brand-new SUV followed her in and turned around before parking. Cavil stepped out, and his face lit up when he spotted me. "Hello, Lily. I hope you don't mind Ann Marie letting me in."

"No problem." I eyed the brand-new SUV. "You already have a car and can drive. Nice."

His eyebrows drew together. "I am a god, Lily. We learn faster than most."

"Thanks for the reminder. I completely forgot what magical type you are."

"You are making fun."

"Yes. You don't need to keep reminding me you're a god."

Humor danced in his eyes. "I know."

"You assholes stay the fuck on the path," came a small voice.

Mom stepped out of her car, stopped, and leaned down. She wagged a finger. When she got done chastising the cussing gnome, she shook her head. "There is something seriously wrong with that gnome. You attract the strangest characters." Her eyes landed on Cavil. "No offense."

I grinned. "We're working on the cussing issue. He can't understand why people find some words offensive and not others."

She shook her head. "Well, he won't be using that language with me if he wants to live. I will not put up with it."

My grin grew wider. "Good luck with that."

I drove Cavil's new car because I knew how to get to Allure. He spent most of the drive on his phone, texting various people and browsing social media. I didn't mind. With him distracted, he wouldn't notice my fidgeting. The supernatural pockets made me nervous, especially Allure, where most of my biological family lived. I usually got harassed at the gate, made a beeline to the warehouse, released some magic, and high-tailed it out of there. I couldn't shake the thought that it was a mistake to help Cavil find a house.

On top of that, I hadn't revealed my magic to anyone outside my family. Between that and the regular hybrid harassment I expected, my nerves were off the charts.

Though, over the last year or so, the new queen tried to change people's minds about hybrids, Allure was still a dangerous place for us. Roman told me to say I belonged to his house if anyone asked, which gave me a little more reassurance. But my stomach still soured as we pulled off onto a logging road in the mountains near the magical gate. I wondered if Cavil would use it as another way to tease me. I hoped not because it was a sore spot.

"Are you okay, Lily?" His velvety voice pulled me out of my thoughts as we made our way down the bumpy road at a snail's pace.

"I'm fine. I always get a little nervous going to Allure. They hate hybrids there."

"Very well. To ease your nerves, I swear I will protect you while you are in Allure today."

I almost lost control of his new car when the zing of the magic contract hit. I stopped where the road washed out and took a few deep breaths as we waited for the magic to test us. "You might want to hold on."

The vegetation changed, and I smashed the gas pedal. We careened off the cliff, hung in the air for a second, and landed on a cobblestone road. A hologram hovered in the air, pointing left, so I followed it to the car storage spell. Inside the spell, an ogre directed us into one of the nearby white mists.

"We're going to have to walk from here." I grabbed my backpack from the back seat, then realized Cavil was already gone.

I found him talking to the ogre just outside of the mist. The guard had an adoring expression on her face as she listened to something he said. Cavil glanced at me, patted the ogre on the shoulder, and pointed toward the gate.

More guards were buzzing around than usual. We joined the short line waiting to get in. "I wonder what's going on."

Cavil's eyes scanned the area. "What do you mean?"

"The guys in purple are palace guards, not gate guards." A silver dragon flew overhead in slow circles and scanned the crowd. It landed and transformed into a woman with long, straight silver hair wearing jeans and a flannel shirt. A vampire blurred by us and stopped in front of her. It looked like they were comparing notes. I clutched my backpack closer. "I don't like this."

Cavil's hand settled on my back. "There have been threats to the pockets, so the queen has stepped up security. We'll be fine."

When we reached the front, a manticore in an enforcer uniform stood behind the shifter who normally manned the gate. His eyes never left me as I scanned my magic into the identification spell. My parents made sure the ID showed me as only a vampire, though most people sensed I was different. The gate guard waved me through without a word and motioned for Cavil to scan. The manticore blocked my path. "What house?"

I swallowed. Let the games begin. "The House of Roman."

"That house is dormant. Give me that bag." He pointed to my backpack.

I handed it over as Cavil joined us, a sour expression on his face. "What is this about?"

I waved a hand as the guy unzipped my backpack and dumped its contents on the ground. I only carried water, a few protein bars, and a change of clothes. "Don't worry about it. It happens to me all the time."

The enforcer sniffed a protein bar and shoved the empty bag back at me. "What house?"

I scooped the contents back into the bag and swung it over my shoulder. "I already told you what house. Not that it matters because it's none of your business." I jerked a thumb toward myself. "I'm not the threat you're looking for."

"Let her go through, Maug," came the voice of reason. I glanced up to see a purple-haired vampire marching toward us. "The books have her listed as Roman's right-hand vampire. You don't want to mess with him. The flashing circle is over there." She pointed to a circular platform swarming with activity. "Flashing without using a circle is against the law."

Cavil took my hand, gave the manticore a fierce look, and dragged me in that direction.

"Thank you," I said to the vampire as I got dragged away by a pissed-off god.

We joined the line of people at the circle. "Flashing circle, eh?" I snickered. "You can tell they don't spend much time in the human world with names like that."

Cavil's eyebrows drew together. "I don't understand the reference."

I scanned the area, listening for danger. "Flashing is when you expose your naked self to strangers."

"Why is that funny? Nudity is a natural thing."

"Humans in this part of the world are a little prudish. Some think public nakedness is wicked. So they don't like it when people wander around without clothes. Or maybe they like it too much." I waved a hand. "Never mind." If you had to explain the joke, it wasn't funny.

Cavil grunted as he scanned the hologram of a map projected next to the line. "Where are we going on your errand? We will take care of that before we meet with my representative."

I pointed to a circle in an industrial part of the city. "That one is the closest."

He eyed the map for a couple more seconds as if memorizing it, then pulled me up the stairs. White light enveloped me, and my stomach threatened to revolt. I squeezed Cavil's hand tighter. When we landed in another circle, he released me.

I bolted down the stairs. I hadn't been transported like that since my biological mother dumped me on Jed when I was twelve. Terrible memories flooded my head, and I needed to move to shake them off.

I glanced at Cavil to see if he noticed, but he didn't comment. His long, sure strides kept up with my skittering steps. I tried to force myself to relax, but the place had me on edge.

I stopped in front of a small warehouse about a hundred yards from the others and held my hand up to the scanner. The door clicked open, and the ozone scent of spent magic drifted out. The lights came on, lighting up a blank concrete room with only a table and chairs on one end and a few practice dummies on the other.

Cavil shut the door with a click. His brow furrowed. "What is this place?"

I wrung my hands. "This is where I let some of my magic out without attracting attention." I pulled off my backpack and moved to the center of the mostly empty room. "I can't use magic in the human world, so I have to come here and release it. Otherwise, it becomes volatile and explodes."

"How often?"

"About once a month."

Cavil folded his arms. "That is not healthy for a being made of magic."

I held up a finger. "Wait until you see it before you judge." I jerked a thumb over my shoulder. "You might want to stand back." The last thing I wanted was to hurt him.

I knew a few defensive spells and usually did each three times before feeling relief. My biological mother only taught me three because it was easier to control me if I stayed ignorant. Jonas and Ann Marie taught me how to improvise so I could do quite a bit more. But I usually stuck with what my mother taught me so I could get it done and get out of Allure.

I took a deep breath as I turned on my sight, reached inside, and un-corked the magic. A golden glow flowed down my arms. With the wave of a hand, I formed a wall across the warehouse and imagined spikes in the floor and ceiling to anchor it. I increased the flow, filled it in, then cut it off and stepped back.

"That's incredible," Cavil said.

I held up a hand. "Wait for it."

As if on cue, giant bloody spikes erupted from it and shot in all direc-tions. I hit the deck, then realized I didn't need to because Cavil conjured a shield around us. He leaned toward the jagged, bloody wall. "Is that some kind of acidic substance?"

I shrugged. "I don't know. It does different stuff every time. The only consistency is that it's always violent and bloody."

"And you have no control over this?"

"No. My biological mother tried to beat it out of me, and my adopted mom tried to figure it out but couldn't."

For the first time since we entered Allure, Cavil smiled. "They are not gods."

I snorted. "Okay, your holiness. What do you suggest?"

He waved a hand, and my wall disappeared. "Let me see what else you can do."

I formed a ball of magic. "This is supposed to be a simple knockout spell." I threw it toward a practice dummy. It turned into a missile and exploded with such force it would have blown up the entire warehouse if Mom hadn't warded it so well. I straightened from my cowering and shook my head. "It's awful."

Cavil eyed the ruined practice dummy. "Try to create a weapon."

"I don't know how to do that. I can improvise in a fight, but only do three spells when practicing. Those two and a box meant to hold people. It turns them into a bloody pulp in ways I wouldn't wish on anyone."

"Only three? Your parents are honorable. Why did they not extend your education?"

"Oh, they tried. The problem is that I can't do my magic at home because it attracts undesirable humans who Roman calls meals. I call them crazies. Also, the police investigate explosions." I pointed at the ruined practice dummy. "It's...I don't know how to explain it. Most mages draw out their magic and can control the flow. I can't. Mine's ingrained into every cell of my body. I can absorb spells in seconds, but they always have a nasty twist at the end when I use them. After a couple of years of fighting human crazies, evading the police, and trying to tame it, we bought this warehouse. It's warded against just about everything."

Cavil nodded. "You are not a mage, so there's no use training like one." He held out his hand. "I am going to teach you how to make a weapon. Don't worry about hurting me or yourself."

Butterflies flittered through my stomach as I took his hand. I felt his magic probing mine as he guided it into creating a spear, then dissipated it. "Pay attention to how I do this. It is creation magic that you can do at will."

I closed my eyes and imagined a spear about six feet long with a long, sharp triangular head, then formed it in my hand. When I opened my eyes and examined the creation, I was extra careful to point it away from Cavil. It looked like I'd imagined it. I eyed the handle. It could use a better grip and was too long for me to use in a fight. Otherwise, it looked good.

I grinned.

The spearhead opened and sprayed blood-red bullets across the warehouse. One pinged off the wall and bounced back toward us, dissipating when it hit Cavil's shield. The smile melted off my face, and my shoulders sunk in defeat. "Told you."

"You need to stop suppressing. You *are* magic, and it does not like to be restrained." He pointed in the direction the bullet went. "It's dark because you're a creature of the night. But you can learn to project what kind of twist it takes. With practice, you will find a dark twist that is not so...."

"Bloody and violent."

"The spear was not nearly as gruesome as the others. You can learn to minimize the volatility by managing your fear and focusing on intention."

Excitement bubbled with the thought that I could control my magic. It wasn't anything Mom hadn't said a million times, but I never believed it. My shoulders slumped when I remembered why. We lived around humans, so I *couldn't* practice more often. "I can't do that, Cavil. Even a warded building in the human world doesn't stop it from luring the crazies."

"Perhaps Ann Marie and I can work together to build you a safe place. I will make myself available for guidance if needed. We will figure this out."

A tiny spark of hope lit inside me. "Okay."

After showing him the gruesome box and practicing a few new tricks with Cavil's guidance, the pressure in my chest eased, and we headed deeper into Allure to look at houses.

CHAPTER ELEVEN

WE LANDED INSIDE A smaller circle on the edge of the most affluent neighborhood in Allure, where two castle guards stood at a heavily warded checkpoint. Both high-powered mages. They ushered us inside a circular area to get our IDs.

A familial tingle stabbed through my chest, coming from two directions. Until then, I tried to convince myself it wasn't stupid to help Cavil. The tingle made me wonder if I'd get in and out without my biological family knowing I was there. I took a deep breath. "Here we go." I handed my backpack to the male guard while a woman tested Cavil's magical ID.

After clearing him, she focused on me with a blank face. "What is your business in this neighborhood?"

I pointed at Cavil. "I'm here to help a friend find a house."

She shoved the magic scanner toward me. "This will identify you if you're in the system."

I held out my hand. "I'm registered."

She eyed the information that appeared in the air skeptically before waving her partner forward. "What do you make of this?"

He shook his head. "Wouldn't be the first time a hybrid tried to fake an ID. This one is a little more absurd than most."

I crossed my arms to keep from throat-punching them. "It's not fake."

The woman shot me the stink-eye. "We shall see." She touched her ear and called for someone.

A couple of minutes later, the knives stabbing through my chest increased, and I had to lock my knees to keep from running. An enormous man with golden hair appeared at the gate on the left. As he drew closer, my eyes grew wider. I was pretty sure the guy was the Regent, Prince Mathias. They called him the bloody prince because he killed anyone who crossed him.

The two guards confirmed my suspicions when they bowed and called him 'Your Majesty.'

He ignored them as his eyes scanned me. The guy had warrior written all over him. It showed in his scarred hands and hard golden eyes. I had never seen someone ooze confidence like he did. He carried himself like he had nothing to prove and would kill me if I so much as sneezed.

I maintained eye contact for too long. After a few seconds, I dropped my eyes to his giant chest. "Sorry, your...uh...sorry."

"I doubt that." His rough voice was laced with a hint of amusement. He turned his attention to the guards. "Show me her ID."

The guard brought it up, and his eyebrows drew together. He focused on me again with a thoughtful expression.

My heart pounded, and I did that too-long eye contact thing again.

He opened his mouth to say something. A loud 'thwap, thwap, thwap' sound assaulted my ears, and he tilted his head toward the sky.

Since he wasn't paying attention to me, I looked up, too. And gasped. The most enormous dragon I'd ever seen flew at us with a speed I couldn't comprehend. While most dragons we'd seen patrolling the skies were one color, this one had black scales tipped with green. His wing beats were so loud I had to cover my ears as he circled once and dropped straight down toward the prince, who didn't even bat an eye. The dragon melted into a hulking, rough man.

My head snapped to Cavil, who watched with a blank face. I knew his magic was ready to strike, but to look at him, you'd never know it.

The prince inclined his head toward the newcomer, then turned his attention back to my ID. The female guard shuffled toward me. "Your Majesty, we think she's a member of the Bellicose or here to start trouble. That ID is obviously fake."

The prince dissipated my ID and eyed me. "Her magic doesn't feel like the Bellicose, although it is strange."

I tore my eyes from him in a respectful amount of time. They landed on the dragon and widened when I recognized the guy as my dad's friend, Drake. "I don't even know what the Bellicose is. And I'm not here to start trouble. The only reason I'm here is to help my friend pick out a house." I waved a hand toward Cavil.

Mind magic tingled inside my head. I had a lot of experience with that, so I put 'Mary had a little lamb' on blast.

Drake grinned. "Hello, Lily. I did not expect to see you here."

My throat closed, and I had to clear it before speaking. How embarrassing. I swore if I got out alive, I'd never go back to the shitty place again. "Hey, Drake. How are you?" I said with as much confidence as I could muster. I switched the song to 'row, row, row your boat.'

"Very well, thank you." He turned to the golden dude. "She's Jonas's adopted daughter and, although she can cleverly disguise her thoughts, is not a threat." He pointed at Cavil. "She sees him as one of her family's rescues and will do anything to help him assimilate into society."

My mouth dropped open. "You got that out of my head, even though..."

Drake chuckled. "No. Jonas spoke of how you rescued a god new to this realm. He's very proud of you and your unusual rescues."

The prince folded his arms. "Your ID says you are from the house of Roman, which is dormant."

I met his eyes for a little too long again. "Yeah. That's a lie, sort of. Roman is rebuilding his house. We formed an alliance to help protect the hybrids." When the prince's stony expression didn't change, I continued. "Look, I get this type of harassment every time I come to Allure. Although, this is the first time they brought someone I'd have a hard time fighting." I realized how hostile that sounded, so I waved a hand. "Never mind. People who can read my magic always ask me what house I belong to. Roman added me as an honorary member to solve the problem. I'm not surprised it didn't. You purebloods are always moving the discrimination goal posts." I realized I was babbling and shut my mouth with a click.

The prince's expression didn't change, but his eyes held respect. "You would make a fine addition to the castle guard."

"Uh. No, thank you. I only want to help Cavil find a house, and then I'll be out of your hair. With such a warm welcome, I have no desire to come back to this neighborhood."

Drake laughed and slapped the prince on the shoulder. Having a good old time at my expense. "She means every word of that."

The prince ignored him as he turned to address the guards. "Jonas the First and the sorceress Ann Marie are her legal parents. They own a house here. Add a resident pass to her ID with my authorization to let her through without question." He gave me one last assessing look, put his hand on Drake's arm, and disappeared.

The guards handed my stuff back and herded us through the checkpoint.

We were a block away before Cavil spoke. "Is what you said true?"

"Which part?"

"That you get harassed when you come to Allure?"

"They're not fond of hybrids here. You would have been better off bringing my parents. They're well-respected, and you could witness the type of ass-kissing you'll receive once you're established."

Cavil fell silent for a few steps. "You deserve much better than that."

"Yeah, well, tell them that."

"I can guarantee you neither of those mages have ever taken a stranger in and helped them establish a life. You have a heart bigger than the moon and at least ten times the power of them. The prince recognized this. Your parents recognized this. You should stand proud and never again cower before lesser beings."

Tears burned my eyes, and I blinked to keep them from falling. If only that were true.

We fell silent as we approached a property with a tall, white wall with generic wards. A witch with long, dark hair stood in front of it. Her face formed into a professional smile. "Cavilourianabalvivelario?" At Cavil's nod, she continued. "I'm your real estate agent, Valerie." She pointed at me. "Your servant can wait out here." The woman ran a device over the latch, and the gates swung open.

"Told you."

Cavil put an arm around my shoulders. Lightning zinged through my body. "Lily is a cherished friend. I suggest you treat her as such."

The witch's face pinched in disgust. "Of course. It's just that she's..." Cavil's sharp whip of magic made her professional mask slip. "Very well, this way."

White stones dotted the landscaping. The building itself was ugly. It looked like a series of white cubes stacked together with slits cut in them for windows. The inside wasn't much better with its modern boxy style. I got bored and opted to stay in the sterile, wide-open great room of the white abyss while Valerie schmoozed Cavil.

The next house was a little better. It reminded me of one of those old houses people had expanded one too many times. Several rooflines with odd angles jutted into the sky, and the layout was awkward, if not dysfunctional. Valerie said an artistic royal couple built it like that on purpose. Something about separating the owner from the peons and guests. To be fair, I was the one who used the word 'peons.' She didn't appreciate it, but I couldn't help poking fun at her.

I was exhausted and annoyed when we got to the third house. Valerie looped her arm through Cavil's as we strolled down the sidewalk. She yapped about something at a million miles per hour. I stayed about ten feet behind them so I didn't rip her lips off and shove them down her throat.

Valerie's eyes sparkled with interest as she smiled up at Cavil. "This is an exquisite property, although not nearly as interesting as the last two."

I dragged my eyes from the pristine stone wall and focused on the house. My heart jumped to my throat when my dream house rose in front of me. The massive Victorian-style house had wrap-around porches and a fancy turret. The powder blue paint was accented with crisp white ornate trim. A sweeping staircase led to the front door. Several chimneys poked up from the roof. It invited me in and screamed, 'home.' I eyed the perfectly placed curved porch before focusing on the landscaping. It looked like it was created in the Victorian period and maintained by gnomes. "Wow."

Cavil tore his attention from the chirping witch. "Do you like this one, Lily?"

I nodded as I pushed past him and darted up the steps, not bothering to hide my vampire speed. The spotless front porch furniture was also white and ornate, with powder blue accents.

Valerie glared at me as she opened the front door. "I chose this house so you could see the contrast. The other houses are much more unique and suit you better."

Cavil put his hand on the small of my back and guided me inside without comment. The large entryway had a built-in bench and coat hooks. Gleaming wooden floors stretched as far as the eyes could see. I couldn't help but smile when I spotted the gorgeous, curved staircase with a hand-carved banister. Though, since we were in a pocket, I supposed it was magic-carved.

I drifted to the old-fashioned kitchen in a dream state. The circular breakfast nook was quaint and inviting, with windows made of unbreakable dragon glass. The magichef, a magical device they used to conjure food in the pockets, looked like an old-fashioned human stove. I couldn't help but think the place was just perfect...for me.

My excitement drained. I wasn't there to find a house for myself. I was there to help Cavil. Valerie thought one of the ugly houses was a better fit for him and was probably right.

I paused as Valerie and Cavil started up the steps to see the second and third floors. "You two go ahead. I'm going to check out the back."

"Don't break anything," Valerie warned.

I stopped to admire the ornate doors before heading out to the porch to lean against the railing. The sprawling back yard looked just as fancy as the front, ending at a massive wall with guards posted on top. The stabbing in my chest that I'd ignored since meeting the prince grew stronger. I realized it was coming from three directions. One sensation was stronger than the others.

Cavil came out the back door, Valerie trailing behind. She was still talking.

"Who lives back there?" I pointed to the back wall.

Valerie's eyes narrowed. "All vampires know who lives there."

My fangs popped out. I retracted them and took a deep breath. "I have an overwhelming urge to rip out your tongue and shove it down your throat just to shut you up, Valerie. So cut the crap and answer my question."

Her eyes grew wide. "That is the house of Umbra, where the Vampire Queen lives."

Cavil gave me one of those sunshine smiles. He liked my darker side. "Will that be a problem for you if I buy this house?"

I examined the stabbing familial recognition in my chest so I wouldn't forget it. "I doubt I'll visit often because of the way these assholes treat me, so it doesn't really matter."

"Leave us." Cavil's order reverberated through my bones, and I turned to comply. He reached out and grabbed my arm to hold me in place.

I heard the back door open and close.

He spread privacy magic around us as I shook off his command. "You love this house."

"I do."

"You don't like the others."

"Nope."

He rubbed his chin. "In my realm, we are all given identical dwellings to serve as shelter. We don't have a personal style and cannot express individuality. It is one reason I left. I found it...restrictive and boring." He shook his head. "There are far fewer colors and types of magic, and it is easy to get overwhelmed here. I need your honest opinion."

"Are you sure? Because humans have a saying about not asking questions if you don't want the answer. And, as annoying as Valerie is, she seems good at her job. Maybe you should ask her."

"Valerie is not the one I trust."

I met his eyes and shook off the shivers when I saw the desperation in them. "The first house looks like a bunch of boxes smashed together. The second one is a hodge-podge of different styles and eras. It gave me a headache. You're way too beautiful to own something that ugly. This one *is* perfect. For me." I moved over to a chair and ran my hand across the back. "But it doesn't matter what I think. If you want to become a power player, you need to decide on what clothes, furniture, and houses will show your status best. There's a lot of judgment around personal style in the upper echelons of society." I waved a hand. "I think you should ignore them and choose things based on what makes you happy instead of what other people think. You are a god, after all." I offered a fake smile. "Do any of these houses sing to you like this one sings to me?"

His eyes scanned my face, his pupils dilating. "Only one thing in this realm sings to me."

I fought not to fidget under the heat of his stare. "And that is?"

He focused on my lips.

Flames lit inside of me, and I locked my knees to keep from jumping him.

He grinned. "I will take your advice and begin thinking more about how things make me feel."

"Good. Great. Okay." I shook out my hands. The guy unbalanced me in a way no one else ever had.

"And I will buy the house that sings to you so I can always remember you helped me build a happy life."

"That's not what I meant."

"It's settled." He released the privacy bubble, took my hand, and dragged me back into the house. "Valerie, I will buy this house today."

They did a bunch of magical contract stuff while I wandered around, admiring the intricate dwarven woodwork and expertly decorated rooms. Most of it came furnished with antique furniture. There were three master suites. The largest one was a little masculine for my taste, with a brown leather sitting area and a chunky four-poster bed. It would work for Cavil, though. I hoped I could visit just to revel in the place's beauty.

When the magical version of the paperwork was complete, Cavil escorted Valerie to the gates. I watched him reset the property and house wards to something that would obscure the view of the vampires and keep everyone else out. I reached forward and touched it as we stepped out. "Nice wards."

He nodded. "Yes."

Leaving Allure was much easier than getting in. We spent the three-hour drive back home talking about interesting things we saw. It was fun.

Until we got to the farmhouse.

I slammed on the brakes. My fangs popped out when I scanned the charred land along the opposite side of the main road. The distinct smell of burned vegetation stung my nose. "Shit. Alex." I threw the car in park and went fluid. I cut through the DMZ and raced across my backyard. And came to a sudden stop.

Mom and Alex sat on the back porch, drinks in hand.

Mom's eyes flicked to Cavil, who popped in behind me. "I take it you noticed the burn marks?"

"What happened? Are you two okay?"

Mom raised her wineglass. "A witch tried to test the wards, and it backfired. His buddies set the grass on fire. They thought we'd leave the wards to put it out."

I grinned. "They didn't do their homework." Mom could do magic with merely a thought and didn't need to be too close for it to work.

"Or they didn't know I'd be here. It's dry this time of year, so I had to borrow some water from the irrigation ditch, or it wouldn't have spread as far as it did. The elf-sprite from the nursery will regrow it in the morning."

I plopped down in a chair. "That's good, I guess."

"Except now they know who Alex is and where he lives."

I held up my phone. "Why didn't you text me?"

Alex set his drink on the table. "There's nothing you could do from Allure besides worry. I cut Cavil a break."

Mom turned her attention to the lurking god. "Cavil, come sit. Do you want something to drink?"

He took the chair next to me. "No, thank you."

"How'd it go? Did you find a house?" Alex asked.

Cavil crossed an ankle over his knee. "I bought the house Lily liked. Gods are taught not to focus on personal style, so I relied on her judgment. I will change that conditioning and begin researching interior decorating to help decide what I like."

Mom nodded. "Lily has excellent taste, so you can't go wrong there. Did you run into any trouble?"

"The pocket's residents treated Lily like a criminal because she is unique and powerful."

"I told him it's normal."

"All hybrids get treated like that, or worse. It's why we live in the human world. The pockets are dangerous to us," Alex explained.

"It turned out okay. Dad's friend Drake vouched for me, and Prince Mathias gave me resident status using your address. I shouldn't have as much trouble next time."

Mom chuckled. "Good luck with that. Your dad is a First and still gets harassed until he puts them in their place." She picked up her phone. "That's a great idea, though. I'll add Alex as a resident, too. So, you met the bloody prince, huh?"

"Yep. He's intense. He told the guards my magic didn't feel like the Bellicose."

Her eyebrows drew together. "Aha. You've solved a problem I've been working on. Can I use your office, Lily?" She didn't wait for me to answer as she rushed through the back door. Mom was a problem solver. Her brain never shut off, and the weirdest things would cause answers to complicated questions to pop into her head. We were used to it.

"Off to solve the world's problems again, eh?"

"Looks like it," Alex mumbled.

Chapter Twelve

"Does this look ripe?" Alex held up a huge apple. He needed to get out of the house, so I agreed to let him go grocery shopping with me. The question reminded me why I rarely took him to the store.

"It's an apple. If it's not ripe now, give it a couple of days."

He turned it over in his hand before wrestling with the produce bags. "I can never get these things to work."

I pulled one off and opened it. "At this rate, we're going to be here all day."

He shook his head. "Apex predators are supposed to be patient when hunting, Lily."

"You're soooo right, Alex. I'll try to remember that the next time I'm stalking an apple in a grocery store."

"Temper, temper." He batted at the grapes as I shoved them into a bag.

I pushed the cart toward the cereal aisle. "We need to take care of those guys who are after you before you lose your mind."

He added sugary cereal to the cart. "Yes, we do."

It took us almost two hours to make our way through the store, and I was ready to snap by the time we got to the self-checkout. Alex insisted on running the items through the scanner while I unloaded and bagged.

As he reached for our receipt, he froze and tilted his head. "We need to leave now."

My hands shook as I grabbed the cart and moved as fast as I could without drawing attention. Alex took it from me when we got outside so

I could enhance my senses. I used my vampire speed to load the groceries while he blocked me from human view. "There's ten of them heading this way fast."

I hit the button to close the hatch. "Let's go."

By the time the back closed, I had the van started. I spotted a black SUV at the other end of the parking lot. "Is that Jed?"

Alex's eyes glazed over. "Yes. He plans to take you by force because you didn't RSVP to that invitation."

I shuddered. "Damn it! I told you we needed to hurry, but noooo. Predators need to be patient." I said the last part in a childish voice.

"It's true, though. Take a right."

I didn't question him because Alex was great at plucking information out of people's heads. I pushed the hands-free phone button. "Call Roman."

It rang once, followed by a female voice. "House of Roman, how may I help you?"

"This is Lily. Tell Roman Jedediah and several vampires tried to kidnap me at the Walmart. We're heading toward I-84 west in Caldwell."

"I will relay the message."

"Sure. He needs to hurry unless he wants to deal with ten dead vampires in his territory." I disconnected and checked the mirror. They followed at a distance. "We need a plan, Alex."

"I'm working on it." His fingers flew over his phone. "Dad's in Allure, and Mom won't reach us in time."

I was grateful for my lightning-fast reflexes as we sped down the side-roads. The cars stayed on our tail. I screeched around the corner of our street and sped up. The SUV behind me tried to clip the back of my van. "Damn it!"

Two cars blocked our gate.

I pulled to the shoulder of the road. "Get behind the wards."

Alex shook his head. "Not without you."

"We can't fight this many vampires."

He hopped out and melted into his lion form.

I flew out the door and went after him.

Vampires spilled out of the cars and lined the road, blocking us from our property.

Jed climbed out of the back of one of the SUVs, straightened his expensive jacket, and smirked. "Hello, Liliana. I wondered if we'd catch you." His eyes flicked to Alex. "Stay out of my head, cat."

Chills ran down my spine at the number of vampires. I glanced down the road to see if Cavil was there, but the farmhouse sat empty. I'd have to use magic. "If he gets to me, flash yourself behind the wards," I whispered as I squared my shoulders. "What do you want, Jed?"

"Tsk, tsk. I've given you plenty of time to do the right thing. I'm afraid I cannot wait any longer." He spread his arms. "You've left me no choice but to insist you come with me. Don't worry. I have a special place for you in my house." His smile sent a chill down my spine. "Take her and kill the cat."

Heart pounding, I turned on my magic sight and threw up a wall between the vampires on the left and Alex. It shot the same blood-red bullets as the spear, taking out three.

Two swept in from the right so fast I didn't have time to react.

One grabbed my arm to throw me over her shoulder. She crumpled to the ground, blood leaking out of her nose and ears. Alex used his size advantage to push me into the freshly restored field across from our house.

I moved my wall to the right. This, I thought. This was why I wanted nothing to do with my biological family. Because they were the worst. I swiped the sheen of sweat from my forehead and flexed my claws. "I'm not going with you, so you might as well piss off back to Allure."

Jed stalked forward, the remaining vampires at his back. Two of them split off to flank us. "You are outnumbered and outclassed. It is futile to fight, Liliana. You will come with me, either willingly or by force."

"I don't think so." I put two vampires in a box. It flashed blood red, and they melted to ash.

Jed didn't even blink at the loss of his people. The asshole.

He raised a hand, and vampires poured out of the nearby fields, some covered from head to toe in weird-looking white suits. I remembered reading those were for the young ones who couldn't tolerate the sun. Alex used his mental magic to drop the younger ones, then dove into the crowd. I created a spear and aimed it at the ones on the other side. It shot bloody darts. "Damn it."

An iron grip wrapped around my ribs. I went limp, rolled, and flipped the vampire over the top of me. The move reversed our positions, so I smashed my elbow into her throat. I was up and running before she quit gurgling. I barreled toward Jed, forming a box around him. It didn't close fast enough, and he went fluid and slipped out.

Blood splattered across my face as Alex dug into someone with a roar. I threw a sleeping spell toward Jed, then extended my claws, went fluid, and stabbed two vampires as they zipped toward my brother.

A sharp pain shot through my whole body as something smashed into me. Claws pierced my stomach. I blinked to clear the black dots from my eyes as I counter-clawed my attacker. Using both hands, I jabbed eight of my ten hand claws into a stomach and curled them so they wouldn't slip out. When my vision cleared, I realized I'd hooked Jed. And his claws were against my throat. A trickle of blood dripped between my boobs. We were in a standoff.

Everyone froze except for Alex, who slunk in behind me.

The vampires who were still conscious moved behind Jed. He smirked. "You have come a long way, daughter."

"I'm not your daughter," I growled. Or at least I tried to. My fangs were still out, so it came out more like, "I vot her otter." I needed to work on that.

"You are very much my daughter, regardless of the drivel Roman has fed you."

The sound of motors roaring stole my attention. Several cars raced toward us, and I spotted the barrel of a gun peeking out of one. As one, Jed and I released each other and hit the dirt.

On my way down, I threw up a wall between us and the street. Two bullets made it through before it formed, one hitting me in the right shoulder and one hitting Jed in the shin. That had to hurt, I thought as I gritted my teeth against my own blinding pain.

My wall shot bullets back at the cars. If I lived, I'd figure out why my magic did that.

Shifters poured out of the cars and fought to get around it. Every time they made a move, I lengthened it, and more bullets shot them. When one tried to climb it and fell, I extended my middle finger.

"Do not be so crass," Jed said.

I punched him in the nose and went fluid to catch up with Alex, who galloped toward my van.

A stream of that dark magic we saw at the apartment complex roared toward us, hit my wall, and exploded. I stretched out a hand and latched onto my brother's mane. He flashed us to the van.

I glanced back and saw the vampires and shifters still working on my wall.

Alex dove into the back seat. I hopped in the driver's side, peeled out, and sped down the rural road. Four cars followed us. "We're in deep shit."

He growled a deep warning growl.

"I knew they were there, so don't eat them." I glanced at the two stowaways in the far back seats, slowed, turned left, and stepped on the gas. The purebloods surrounded our property, and Jed wouldn't stop until he got what he wanted. Especially now that he knew I could be used as a weapon. I winced at the thought of how he'd expect me to use my magic. "Where should we go?" I could protect Alex from one threat, but not while I had to watch my own ass. "Should we head to Mom and Dad's place?" I didn't want to drag our trouble there, but our options were limited.

Alex melted into his human form and dug through a bag, looking for clothes. "No. I hate to say it, but we need to follow Mom's instructions and go to Allure."

"Nope."

"I don't see any other option. They have our house surrounded. All they have to do is wait until we run out of food. Allure's a big city, and we could get lost in the crowds."

I tapped the steering wheel and checked the mirrors. I so did not want to go to Allure, but he was right. If we could find a safe place, it would give us time. "Fine. Text Mom."

"Mistress," the male stowaway said.

"You two trying to defect from good ole Jed's house, or are you spies?"

The female stowaway didn't take her eyes off Alex. "The former. You're the only vampire aside from the Queen who can break his hold."

"Not true and not the time." Stray vampires were the last thing I needed.

The people following us weren't vampires. They were those purebloods who wanted Alex. Those guys didn't know the roads like I did, so it only took a few minutes for me to lose them. I didn't slow as I skidded around the corner and barreled down the two-lane highway that led toward the mountains.

When we got far enough away, I glanced in the rearview mirror and addressed the stowaways. "What's your deal?"

The male vampire fought a smile. "We want to join your house."

"I don't have a house."

"You should," the female said.

I'd had enough bullshit for one day, so I shot her a look Mom used on me when I tried to get one over on her. "You have until we get to Allure before I ditch you, so cut the crap. I get that you want to escape from Jed's house because who wouldn't? He's a complete asshat. But I'm going to need more."

The guy cleared his throat. "I hate Master Jedediah."

"Everyone hates good ole Jed. How did you defect?"

They shared a look.

The man sighed. "We snuck a taste of your blood during the fight. It dulls his hold on us."

I tightened my grip on the steering wheel to keep my anger from exploding. "Look. I'm a hybrid, not a House Master. I don't have any desire to be one. So, you can't stay with me." Plus, I didn't want the added responsibility. I wanted to save my brother and look for a new toxic workplace, not play politics.

The woman frowned. "That's not true, Mistress."

"Lily. Not Mistress or any other bullshit title the purebloods made up. And it's true. I'm only thirty. And I'm not even sure I'm a natural-born vampire. So you'll have to move to Roman's house or petition the Vampire Queen for a transfer."

Chapter Thirteen

My stomach soured as I pulled into the parking spell outside Allure just after dark. The three passengers had been unusually quiet. Mom texted Alex and said she'd handle the clean-up at our house and send our personal items once we got settled. It felt like our parents were abandoning us. Something we both had experience with.

Alex's mage mom sold him to a pack of wolves when he was five. They had him for two weeks, using him as a practice dummy to teach their kids how to fight. His lion family pulled him out and dumped him on us a few months after they adopted me. We all fell in love with the sweet little guy. Mom was our miracle. She was great at helping us work through our issues. That and Dad's insistence on honesty with ourselves and each other made us well-adjusted adults despite our rocky starts.

I eyed the gate. "This sucks."

"Yeah." Alex ran a hand through his hair. "Let the games begin."

We strode toward the gate with the vampires trailing behind. There was way more security than when Cavil and I went through. Two dragons flew in a zigzag pattern overhead, one peach-colored, the other dull gray. There wasn't a line to get in, so eight gate guards scanned our bloody clothes. I pretended I didn't notice them and focused on a team of enforcers digging through the filthy bags carried by a couple of banshees.

Alex and I scanned our magic IDs and tried to act casual.

I rubbed my sweaty hands on my pants. "What's with all the security?"

The guard turned her hard eyes to me. "That is none of your concern."

"Hey, Alex, remember when Dad said we'd be treated better now?"

"Stop stirring the pot, Lily." His voice was serious, but I caught the sparkle of humor in his eyes.

The guard's eyes narrowed when my ID materialized in front of her. "Where did you get this ID?"

"Originally? Or when it got updated?"

"Both."

"My dad, Jonas the First, brought me here to get an ID when I was a kid. The upgrade happened a couple of weeks ago when I entered my parent's neighborhood with a friend. The palace guard called the regent because of my odd magic. He cleared me and updated the ID." I hoped the name-dropping would speed things along.

The guard rolled her eyes and pointed to an area inside the gate where Alex waited. "Wait over there." She motioned toward the vampires. "Who are they?"

"They're stowaways who claim their House Master abuses them. They need to be sent to the Vampire Queen."

The enforcer made a hand signal. Five vampires zipped by and took off with them. Neat trick, that.

"You're free to go," a castle guard said.

As we left, I pointed to the flashing circle. "Do you know what those are called?"

"I'm not in the mood."

"Flashing circles. Where people can legally flash each other." I pretended to open a trench coat. "Do you think you can *flash* us downtown so we can get there faster?"

Alex went to push his glasses up and almost poked himself in the eye. Wearing glasses helped him fit in among humans, but he'd stand out like a sore thumb wearing them in Allure. "Yes. Or I could take myself and make you walk. Are we getting a hotel or going to Mom and Dad's house?"

He knew I button-pushed when I got nervous, but it still annoyed him. I held up my phone. "Mom said not to go to their house. Let's try to get a hotel. If they reject us, we can crash at the warehouse tonight, or maybe Cavil's new house if he's there."

"This is stupid."

"I agree." Our parents planned everything to the letter. Sending us in a general direction with vague instructions wasn't like them. Something had them spooked. "Mom knows something that she's not telling us."

"Yes. And I couldn't get it out of her head. I suppose she has her reasons." He stepped into the circle and held out his arm.

We landed downtown in a gigantic town square that held two of the largest circles I'd ever seen. Supernaturals of all types hustled in and out of them. A town square of old-fashioned brick and stone buildings that contained both businesses and housing surrounded the circles. Cobblestone streets branched off in every direction, adding to the old-world charm.

"This is beautiful," I said as Alex led us down an alley. Or a street. They were all narrow, so I couldn't tell the difference.

"It's okay." He pointed right when we emerged from the town square. "There's four or five hotels down there."

A bear family in animal form sauntered down the other side of the street, the mom in front, the dad in back, with three cubs bouncing between them. An ogre stepped out of a shop and handed the mom a bag of something with a smile. I loved how supernaturals had a place where they could be themselves and hoped that one day, the hybrids could find a similar setup.

I was lost in the city's wonders when I noticed the name of a building and came to a sudden stop. "What the..."

"Can you make fun of the business names later? Maybe after we have a place to stay?"

I shrugged. "I'm having a hard time with the disconnect. Do they really think PISD is a fantastic name for an organization? I wonder if everyone who works there is really angry. Garrr." I fake-growled.

Alex didn't comment.

The first hotel we stopped at was super fancy. The doorman, a giant with way too many muscles, barred our way. "We don't take your kind here."

My face flushed with anger.

Alex dragged me away. "These people are stupid to ignore the power and ingenuity hybrids could bring to their society, so the jokes on them."

By the time we got rejected by the third hotel, I'd stopped making fun of the businesses and their strange names. Instead, I started making plans to turn the warehouse into a temporary place to stay. It had a bathroom with a shower, but we'd need beds and a way to get food. It had the advantage of being heavily warded. The only problem was that it could be traced back to us. Which meant Jed most likely knew about it.

The last hotel on the street sat right across from a wrecked building. Repairs were underway, but the top floor was still a shell. A bronze dragon perched on top of it, power radiating off her in waves.

Dragons of all colors circled her. A deep blue wingless dragon slithered around the ruined building and roared at an orange one who coiled into a ball and sputtered fire. It had to be their headquarters.

The idea of staying that close to the majestic creatures was exciting. "What do you suppose happened here?"

Alex tilted his head back and frowned. "Looks like a bomb. Do you think those guys are after the dragons for their mental magic?"

"I doubt it. Dragons are too powerful. Maybe we shouldn't try to get a room here."

A black dragon circled the bronze one and landed on what was left of a massive balcony that jutted out from a floor just below her.

"It beats the warehouse. Let's try. The worst they can say is no."

I turned back to the hotel. It was fancy, so I doubted they'd let us in. "They're dragons. The worst they could do is kill us."

"They look like they have their own problems. Two hybrids aren't even going to register as a blip on their radar."

"Fine."

The doorman's bright yellow eyes scanned us as we approached. They settled on me. "You a vampire?"

"Yes. House of Roman."

He swiped his long yellow hair out of his eyes. "I heard Roman was rebuilding his house. That drama must be fun to watch."

A guy after my own heart. "He keeps stealing vampires from Jedediah."

He threw his head back and laughed, then opened the door. Alex latched on to my arm and dragged me through.

It was clear by the clientele that the hotel catered only to dragons. I didn't see a single non-dragon in the lobby other than us. It would be a great place to hide out. No one would expect a couple of hybrids there. I wondered if I could befriend some of them. If they liked us, they'd keep my brother safe.

Alex dragged me to the front desk and set down his bag. The dragon behind the counter leaned forward and assessed us with freaky white eyes. "What brings a couple of powerful hybrids to our establishment?"

"We'd like a room for a couple of weeks." Alex used his professional voice.

The dragon focused on me. "Is that right? Are you a mated pair, then?"

"No." We answered at the same time.

Amusement danced in his glowing white eyes. "If you're here to cause trouble, you'll die. We will not go against the Crown."

My eyes narrowed. "You're a white dragon?"

"I am."

"Been to West Boise lately?"

He bared his teeth. "What kind of trouble are you in, little vamp?"

I shook out of Alex's death grip. "We're not in trouble with anyone in this pocket. No one else will give us a room because we're hybrids. If you don't want to help, just say so. We're used to being rejected by purebloods."

The dragon didn't laugh or take me up on my offer to throw us out like I'd expected. Instead, the humor drained from his face. "You have the heart of a warrior, young one." He turned his attention to some kind of magical device I'd never seen before, then held out a standard ID checker. "I will need you to submit to an ID check. It is difficult to lie to a dragon, but it does happen."

Alex and I shared a look, and he presented his ID. The dragon read it without comment, then waved for me to go. When mine came up, he pulled out two round discs. "Since you are siblings, we shall give you adjoining rooms. Do not cause trouble, and you can stay as long as you like. Cause trouble, and we will kill you." He leaned forward and flashed a predatory smile.

My chest tightened, and I swallowed. I didn't doubt the threat was real.

"Right. Thank you, Sir Dragon." Alex shoved me toward the strange magical elevators.

Our rooms were on the seventh floor. One room had a bed so big it would easily fit four people. The other had two king-sized beds. All three had blue and gold paisley blankets and a mound of pillows. The plush blue carpet was squishy under my feet as I checked out the identical marble bathrooms with jacuzzi-sized bathtubs and colossal walk-in showers.

The balconies had two cozy-looking chairs and a small table. No railings. Just inside the balcony doors, the rooms had a table with four chairs and a massive magichef. I'd only ever seen them on the maginet.

I opened a closet and grinned when I saw a device that would clean and press our clothes. "This place is great."

Alex set his bag on the colossal bed in the single room and headed straight to the magichef. "I call dibs on this room."

"Fine with me." I headed to the room with two beds and threw open the balcony doors. A cool fall breeze floated in, carrying the smell of street food and something floral. A tan dragon launched from the building across the street. I needed food and sleep, or I could have enjoyed the view for hours. Our situation was looking up.

I jerked out of a sound sleep, went fluid, and fell on my ass. When I slept, it was so sound that it took me a few minutes to come out of it.

I kicked the blankets off my legs as I stood. A powerful dragon was outside my room. Adrenaline shot through me, and it took a few seconds to get the shaking under control.

The pounding sounded again.

I stomped to the door and swung it open.

A pair a black eyes swept over me, and I realized I only wore a crop-top and my underwear.

He didn't seem to care as he focused on my face. "Liliana First?"

I blinked. "It's Lily. And you are?"

"Bastien."

"I'm going to go out on a limb and say you're here because we're a couple of hybrids staying at a hotel reserved for dragons?"

His face turned to stone. "Dragons don't share those weak-minded ideals. The Queen of Ahl asked my mother, the Dragon Queen, to take you in. Glacintial informed me two powerful hybrids checked into the hotel last night. I wanted to meet you."

"So, my parents arranged for us to stay here?" Mom didn't tell me that. She only said to find a hotel.

"Correct. May I come in?"

I stepped aside. "Heard you were matched with a witch. How do you navigate the discrimination?" I held up a hand when my brain engaged. Not a good idea to piss off our hosts. "Never mind. It's different for royalty, eh?" I shut the door and headed to the magic chef without bothering to put more clothes on. He was there to throw me off my game. I could do the same. "You want something to drink?"

The dragon strolled over to the balcony door and opened the curtains. "Explain why you need shelter."

"Not one for chitchat, eh? No one else would rent us a room. If you want us out of your hair, that's fine."

"We promised to shelter you, and we will. I want to talk to the mental mage hybrid."

I moved to stand between him and the door to Alex's room. "People in hell want ice water. I doubt they'll get it."

His lip quirked. "You have human values. Interesting."

"No. But I know a plethora of their cliches."

He bared his teeth. "You and my cousin will get along well. Though that is a lot of bravado from a puny snack seeking shelter."

"I already told you we'd move on. We don't want charity or protection from you or any other pureblood."

"It's okay, Lily." Alex's voice came from behind me.

"Damn it, Alex. Why can't you let me protect you for once?"

He ignored me. "I'm Alexander First. I go by Alex, not the mental mage hybrid. What can we do for you, Prince Bastien?"

I was going to have a talk with the little snot later about his ass-kissing. And give him a high-five for the snarky name comment.

Bastien inclined his head. "I understand the Bellicose are trying to recruit you."

"If you're referring to the group that goes by the name Sentinels and consider their plan to kill my sister to get to me as recruiting, then yes."

Bastien rubbed his chin. "I doubt your sister is easy to kill, even though your mental shields keep me from reading her."

"You assume right," Alex answered, not taking the information-gathering bait.

The prince turned his black eyes to me. "What are you hoping to accomplish here?"

I threw on a fluffy hotel robe. "The only reason I'm here is because we're being targeted by two groups. Vampires and those guys with the nasty magic. My brother is more important to me than causing trouble. We plan to blend in and draw as little attention as possible."

Alex nodded. "Hybrids stick out like sore thumbs inside the pockets. Lily more than most. But we'll try not to cause trouble."

The dragon squared his shoulders. "Very well. The throne of Devarkalara offers you sanctuary at our hotel for the duration of your stay. Should the Bellicose try to get to you while in this establishment, we will eliminate them." He held out an envelope. "Is this the vampire who is causing you trouble?"

I snatched it out of his hand and ripped it open, read the contents, then handed it to Alex. "Where did you get that?"

"A vampire handed it to the doorman just after you arrived."

I rubbed my face. The dragons were sheltering us as a favor to Mom, and I didn't want to insult them. I also didn't want them to have to deal with Jed. It could start a war. "Jedediah thinks I belong to him. I don't." I pointed at the envelope. "He sent me a dinner invitation that I ignored. This is a reminder that I'm required to attend. I'll accept it, so you guys don't need to deal with them."

His black eyes sparkled with humor. "I see."

"You don't. But that's okay. I'll handle the vampires."

"You do that." He moved toward the door. "I do not expect you to go against your mischievous nature as a condition of staying here, Lily. However, should you start a war with the vampires, I will throw you out on your ass."

The door shut with a click.

I shook my head. "Well, that was terrifying."

"It's like he knows you can't help yourself."

Which meant I needed to work extra hard to stay hidden.

We stayed at the hotel for an entire day. Then we left to wonder through the nearby supernatural shops. I held the door to a candy shop open for

Alex in his lion form. "You sure you don't want to walk around naked? Because that's okay, too."

He huffed, trotted down the street, and stopped in front of a deli.

"Nope. I'm not eating lunch with a lion." Tingling between my shoulder blades told me we were being watched. I scanned the crowded street, but there were too many people. "Maybe we should get our food to go."

He pushed through the door, and I shuffled inside behind him. The scent of pickles and freshly baked bread made my stomach growl. I pasted on a congenial smile as we approached the counter.

A leprechaun grinned as we approached. "Hello. I haven't seen you in here before."

"We're just visiting. Can we get four specials to go, please?"

He eyed Alex. "That is an odd-looking lion shifter."

"He's an american lion. They're bigger and darker than modern lions." It was a practiced answer. People always commented on Alex's appearance.

"I see. So what brings you here?"

"Our parents insisted we visit."

He nodded as he pushed buttons on the magichef. "There's been some unrest, so watch your backs."

"We will."

He packaged the sandwiches using a magical device and set them on the counter.

As I paid, I glanced toward the door. A minotaur came in with a pixie sitting on his shoulder. Maybe mixed magic couples were welcome in downtown Allure. "Thanks," I mumbled as I took the food.

"Come back anytime."

The deli wasn't the only shop that welcomed us, but it was nice to know we could get food somewhere outside the hotel. Not that we needed to. The magichefs were well-stocked.

The door guard eyed our bags. "Where did you get that?"

"At the deli down the street."

"Ah, Thaddeous's place. His sandwiches are acceptable." He leaned forward. "But I wouldn't make a habit of bringing it here. Dragons take as much pride in their culinary skills as they do their drinking."

The guy was once again speaking my language. "No kidding?"

He nodded as he swung the door open. "In you go."

The bar on the hotel's first floor was full of dragons when I slunk down after Alex went to bed. I hoped to befriend one and find more information about the purebloods chasing us. We heard people discussing a battle in Allure a few days before we arrived, and I wanted to know more.

I'd never met a hybrid dragon, but I knew they existed. Otherwise, they'd be a bunch of inbred dolts. One thing was for sure, they were fascinating.

Every head turned my way as I entered the bar. A stool between a red dragon and a purple one sat empty, so I headed that way.

The silver-haired bartender raised an eyebrow as I took a seat. Dale had me trained to accept whatever drink he put in front of me. It caused me to hesitate to make an order. I pasted on my most congenial smile and pretended not to notice the dragon's wince. "I'll have a vodka tonic, please."

He waved his hand, and it appeared in front of me. "Let me know when you need a refill. Good luck." He turned and walked away.

I eyed the drink. "Well, that's handy."

The purple dragon beside me chuckled. "You ain't seen nothing yet. Wait until some of these idiots get drunk and conjure a feast."

I bit back a smile. It sounded like a good time to me. "You can do that?"

Her purple eyes scanned me, sending a shiver down my spine. "No. Not everyone has culinary magic, but it is a common ability. What about you? What can you do?"

"A lot. I have it on good authority that I'm a powerful vampire. My magic is gruesome, so I don't use it often."

Her grin was predatory. "I have the urge to ask for a demonstration."

"You really don't want one." I took a sip of my drink. "What happened to the building across the street?"

The smile melted off her face. "We had a traitor."

The red dragon on the other side of me cleared his throat. "Not another word, June."

My head whipped to him. "Was it the guys with the black magic?"

He raised an eyebrow.

I waved a hand. "You don't need to tell me. I stole a ton of information out of an office in Boise. I know what they're up to."

"No shit?" The purple dragon asked.

"Not a single one. They want to overthrow the Queen, enslave hybrids, then take over the entire world."

"Ah, the usual," the red dragon mumbled.

"Yep. You'd think the bad guys would get more creative as we evolve, but no."

He waved his hand, and another drink appeared in front of me. "One would think."

I eyed the drink. "Why come to a bar if you can make your own drinks?"

The purple dragon, June, grinned. "Like vampires, dragons are social creatures."

"Right."

The red dragon leaned into my personal space. "What are you doing staying in this hotel, little vampire?"

I elbowed him a little harder than I needed to. "Hiding my brother and drinking."

He threw his head back and laughed. "That's not what I heard."

My heart sank. I needed to find out why Mom sent us there. She had to have a reason other than just keeping us safe. It wasn't like her to shield us from danger.

I learned a lot about dragons that night. Their friendliness and loyalty were as remarkable as their fierceness. June, the purple dragon, worked security at Dragon Headquarters across the street and had a lot of fun stories. The red dragon did patrols and had been an integral part of a recent battle. He said the group who chased us was everywhere, and it was hard to tell a friend from a foe.

As I stumbled to my room in the wee hours of the morning, I thought a lot about what he said. What if hybrids were working with them to help enslave us? If so, we were in more trouble than I thought. We needed to do something other than sit in a hotel, drink, and eat delicious food like a couple of gluttons.

CHAPTER FOURTEEN

"THIS IS A BAD idea," Alex said as we made our way to the neighborhood where Cavil bought his house.

I wanted to see what happened to the castle and gawk at the Victorian mansion again. "It'll be fine. We'll walk by Cavil's house and get out of here."

"Still not a good idea. I smell vampires in this neighborhood. A lot of them."

A tingling between my shoulder blades made me slow down and scan the street. "It's fine. They won't even know we're here."

When we arrived, the same two guards were at the neighborhood gate. "You're back, huh?" the woman who called the prince asked. "And you brought a new friend."

I jerked my thumb toward Alex. "This is my brother, Alex First. Jonas and Ann Marie's other adopted hybrid child. I'm throwing it out there, so maybe you'll speed up the inevitable harassment. We'd like to get on with our day."

"Funny." She held up the magic ID scanner. "Scan, please." She read our IDs and waved us through.

My eyes widened as we passed the castle. The entire front of it was flattened. Several mages surrounded it, making repairs using magic. Griffins, both shifted and in human form, swarmed around them. Gargoyles lined the wall outside, with more griffins and palace guards filling the gaps between them. "What happened to the castle?"

"The Bellicose tried to destroy it during the battle," the guard answered.

"Is everyone okay?"

"There were a few casualties, but the royal family is fine."

I focused on the familial stabbing in my chest. The sensation came from three directions, including two inside the neighborhood. "My condolences."

"Thank you."

Alex and I trudged past the castle ruins and took the next right. I pointed left. "Mom and Dad's house is that way, across the street from the Shifter Alphas. Cavil is about a mile straight up the road. It backs up to the Vampire Queen's place."

He scanned the area as we walked. "This is a terrible idea."

"We're fine. They didn't show up when I was here before, so maybe they can't sense me."

"Roman can, so they can. If anything happens, I'm going to tell you I told you so every chance I get for the next hundred years."

"Nothing's going to happen. We'll get in and out."

We reached the gates of Cavil's house, and I touched the wards, the supernatural equivalent of a doorbell. A witch emerged. Her long blonde hair bounced, and her heels clicked as she strode down the walkway. She stopped and scanned us. "Can I help you?"

"Is Cavil around?"

"The God Cavil is unavailable." Her tone suggested we were garbage and not worth his time.

I fought to keep my fangs from springing out.

Alex latched onto my arm. "Come on, Lily. She thinks hybrids are scum."

My shoulders slumped. "I really wanted to show you the house. It's amazing."

"You have no business here, so vacate the premises," the witch ordered.

I followed Alex without acknowledging her. It was the best way to deal with pureblood haters when I didn't feel like fighting. "I guess I have to make an appointment to see him now that he's Mr. Important."

Alex pulled me into the shade. "Text him like you should have done before we came all the way out here."

I leaned against a tree and pulled out my phone. "Fine. But after we leave, we're staying near the dragons. The rest of this pocket sucks."

It didn't take long for Cavil to appear at the gate. He said something to the witch that I didn't bother to listen to, then swung it open. "Come in."

A wave of anticipation washed over me at the sight of him. He looked and felt like sunshine after a storm. "Hello, Your Holiness. Aren't you extra gorgeous today?"

His blue eyes sparkled with humor as he motioned us inside. "You flatter me."

"Oh, please. Everyone knows you're a pretty god. I'm just stating the obvious."

He offered me his arm, and I took it as we strolled up the walkway, Alex trailing behind. "I heard you were part of a recent battle."

"Which one?"

He stopped at the top of the steps. "The one at your house. Building my staff is taking all my time. I apologize for not being there to help you."

"World domination isn't all it's cracked up to be, eh?"

"I don't know what 'cracked up to be' means."

"It's not what you expected."

"I am no longer sure if building power is what I want to do."

"Then don't. You're a god, after all. You already have a beautiful witch to turn friends away. What more do you need?"

"She should not have done that. You can come and go as you please. It won't happen again."

"We're used to it," Alex said. "How is that portfolio working for you?"

"Very well. You are a financial genius." He led us through the door and into a receiving room.

I froze. The old-world charm was gone, replaced with white on white on white. Two gigantic modern white leather sectionals occupied the center. White frames adorned the white walls and held barely there pastel still-life paintings. Even the wooden floors were whitewashed. I wanted to burst into tears. "What did you do to this place?"

"Do you like it?"

I hated it. It made me want to take a paintbrush and fling it around to help the dead room come back to life. I took a deep breath, then another, and reminded myself it wasn't my business. "It doesn't matter what I think. Do you like it?" I glanced around again, trying to keep my face neutral.

Alex raised his hand to push up his nonexistent glasses, then dropped it. "Where did you get the white-on-white idea? Is that normal for your realm?"

"No. My realm is more monochrome, with grays, blacks, and whites, but not like this. I got it from the human internet."

"And you like it?" I couldn't keep the disgust out of my voice.

"This is the correct style for the times, is it not?"

"Right. Um. Can I make a suggestion?"

Cavil took my arm and dragged me toward a white bar with white quartz countertops. "Of course."

I took the water he offered. "Skip what's trendy and decorate based on what makes you happy. I'm not trying to tell you what to do, but you're the one who lives here. Choose colors you like."

His frown was as potent as his smile. "So you don't like it."

Alex smirked. "It's like a blank canvas."

"I liked it the way it was when we looked at the house." I held up a hand. "Like I said, it's not my house, though. It's yours, so do what makes you happy."

His eyes swept the room. "Very well. I will think about it."

I realized I'd made him second guess himself and waved a hand. "Never mind. White's great."

His lips twitched at the blatant lie. "I like your advice."

Alex chuckled. "That makes one person."

"You need to stop liking it. This is your world domination plan and your cult. Ignore me."

He threw his head back and laughed. "You are a true gem, Lily."

"She's something," Alex mumbled. "What do you know about the group trying to take over the coalition?"

Cavil's face grew serious. "I don't fully understand what is happening. The First Drake requested I help the Queen with her...some things, so I will try to get more information. When I find out more, I will flash to you or use my device to text."

I held up a hand. "You can't flash without using the circles here, so that might not be a good idea."

"That is a safety measure for mages. I am a god. I can go anywhere without leaving a trail like they do."

I blinked. "Okay."

He focused on Alex. "How is your stay in this fine pocket?"

When we left Cavil's house, Alex stopped and peered down the street leading to the Vampire Queen's house. "What do you want to bet the queen doesn't know Jedediah invited you to dinner?"

I rubbed my stomach. "It was in her writing. I think. But I'm not taking that bet. If she gets her hooks into me, I doubt I'll live to see another day." A vampire zipped toward us from the opposite direction. We moved out of the way, and I hopped behind a tree. "We should go."

Alex's eyes scanned the street. "A group of shifters is waiting for us near that checkpoint."

I sucked in a breath. "They know we're here. Should we go to Mom and Dad's place? Or maybe ask Cavil to hide us?"

"No. I picked up some following us yesterday, but a dragon always hovered around us while we shopped. We don't have backup out here."

Two more vampires came from the direction of the checkpoint. "And we promised to stay out of trouble." I pulled my phone out. "Did they follow us here? Is Cavil in trouble?"

"He can take care of himself."

A group of three vampires zipped down the street. One stopped at the corner and cocked his head in our direction. "You there. Come out from behind that tree." His buddies joined him.

"We need to get out of here now." I slammed a hand on Alex and took off in the opposite direction.

The vampires followed as I swung down another street toward the house our parents owned. I'd never been there because they used it as a couple's retreat, but I knew where it was. Sort of.

More vampires zipped toward us from that direction, so I took a right and swung down a winding road, then lost all sense of direction. I weaved between wards and popped out on another street.

I screeched to a halt near a flashing circle and bent over to catch my breath. "Flash us back downtown."

Alex's eyes went wide as he focused on something behind me.

Heart pounding, I turned in slow motion. "Shit. Alex, we're going to have to hit and run."

My brother shook his head. "Calm down, Lily. It's fine. We didn't do anything, but if we run, they'll think we did."

I took a shaky breath and focused on the blood relation feeling that came from several directions. "We're so screwed."

In the blink of an eye, five vampires surrounded us. A woman with short brown hair and purple highlights spoke. "What house are you from?"

I cleared my dry throat. "The House of Roman. We were visiting a friend. Not that it's any of your business."

Her eyes narrowed. "Roman is dormant."

"He's not." Alex's voice was calm and confident. "We're leaving..."

A vampire behind me yanked my braid.

My fight or flight kicked in. I threw my elbow back and went fluid as my claws and fangs snapped out. I didn't want to kill the vampires, or we'd never get out alive. So, I went low and used my claws to cut tendons.

Another guard tried to jump in, and he sunk to his knees, holding his head.

My heart galloped as several more vampires rushed towards us. "Shit."

The purple-haired woman charged, ramming into me. We tumbled, rolling over a few more vampires like a couple of bowling balls. I used my toe claws to do as much damage to them as possible.

She was every bit as vicious as me, I realized, as she bit my shoulder and slammed her claws into my thigh.

I elbowed her in the ribs and kicked her shins with my foot claws, then used my four fangs and gnawed on her shoulder.

She clawed at my face. I blocked with one hand and stabbed her stomach with the other. We released each other, jumped away, and crouched simultaneously.

Alex didn't shift. Instead, he used his mental magic as he dropped anyone who tried to restrain him. They caught on, and a guy picked up a rock and threw it at him.

"No!" I screamed.

A fist smashed into the side of my head. I broke the offending arm while I waited for the black dots to clear from my vision. The purple-haired bitch charged again. I went fluid to get out of her way, then pinged off someone who reached out to grab me. I dove toward their knees and kicked out, catching purple-hair's stomach.

They decided it was dog pile on Lily time. So many piled on me that I couldn't move. "Alright, alright. I give. Holy hell. Can't a girl go for a walk with her brother in these asshole pockets? Alex, are you okay?"

"Ugngh." He'd be fine.

Purple hair got me into some kind of headlock as a man in a very expensive, pristine suit slunk to the front of the crowd. He froze. His dark blue eyes flicked to Alex and returned to me. The familial tingling in my chest went nuts.

A woman with multi-colored hair and a shit-ton of power pushed past him, followed by the most beautiful woman I'd ever seen.

Powerhouse eyed me before turning her attention to Alex. I didn't need the stabbing in my chest to tell me we were related. Her hair alone gave it away with its chunks of gold and red. Though I only had one chunk of each. I knew exactly who and what she was. The person I'd tried to avoid my whole life. The person my biological mother tried to turn me into. Tears sprang to my eyes, and I blinked them back. Alex was right. Going to see Cavil was a stupid idea.

Powerhouse moved toward him.

I lost my shit and thrashed against the guards. "Don't you touch him. We didn't do anything."

"Relax before you make the situation worse. That guy needs a healer." She pointed at my brother. She reached out and touched him. His wounds instantly melted away and his skin took on a healthy glow.

The woman nodded once, then turned her attention to me. "Do you need my help?"

I did the fish mouth thing before gathering my wits. "Who the hell are you, and why are these vampires attacking us?"

"She's a rogue who claimed to be from a dormant house, Your Grace." Purple hair squeezed my neck a little tighter.

I fought the urge to start fighting again. Something about Perfect Suit's eyes told me it would not end well for me.

Powerhouse crouched in front of me. My eyes watered from the enormous amount of power radiating from her. I tried not to flinch as her golden eyes examined me. "She's not feral. She's got a lot of power, though. You can let her go if she promises not to attack." She raised a perfect eyebrow.

I let out a breath and resigned myself to the torture that was to come. It was always that good of a time when I met blood relatives. There'd be no way I could fight her and win. "I'll do whatever. Just let my brother go. He has nothing to do with this."

"It's not my call. You're in vampire territory, so it's up to Ara, though I doubt she'd harm Jonas's kids." She motioned to the tiny woman gliding through the crowd. "A word of advice. Watch your language around her. She's not fond of swearing."

I tried to school my face. "No Problem."

The woman stood. "Hey, Ara. I think we found your granddaughter."

The world dropped out from under me.

Chapter Fifteen

Someone patted my arm. "It's okay, dear. Come, let's have some tea and talk."

I blinked at the tiny woman hovering over me, a lock of straight black hair dangling over her shoulder. I recognized her as the vampire from the bar and wrenched myself into a sitting position. "What?"

She took my hand, pulled me to my feet with too much strength, and linked her arm through mine. I swung my head around until I spotted Alex. He walked next to the woman who had healed him. My shoulders sagged in relief.

They stiffened again as Perfect Suit stepped to my other side.

I rubbed my temple. "We were just out for a walk."

The woman patted my hand. "We only wish to have a chat, dear."

I swallowed back bile. Chats with my biological family always ended with someone in pain. Usually me. "No offense, but I don't have a great track record with vampires who want to chat, especially ones who…" I cut off.

"Are family," she finished for me. "Yes. I understand you had quite an interesting upbringing. That's part of what we would like to chat about."

"Look, if you're going to torture me, at least let my brother go. He has nothing to do with this."

Rage flashed across her face. She closed her eyes and shook her head. "I am sorry your impression of us is so negative. I am especially sorry that my son is responsible for it." She patted my hand again. "I promise you and your brother will not be harmed in my territory by anyone under my control."

The magic contract zinged through me. "Whoa."

"It's okay, Lily," Alex said. "None of these people want to hurt us."

Perfect Suit swung toward him so fast I flinched. "Stay out of our heads."

Alex held up his hands. "Sorry. Habit." He was, in fact, not sorry. Perfect Suit knew it, too, but he didn't comment.

Our procession passed a sweeping staircase and entered a comfortable sitting room done in muted yet tasteful colors. The Vampire Queen led us to a cozy old-world sitting area in front of a stone fireplace. The room had enough antique chairs for a large group to gather and enjoy a cocktail after dinner.

I scanned the other end of the room. Two sofas faced a bank of windows. Some kind of magic covered them to keep the sunlight out and reflected a mountain scene. "Wow. This house is amazing."

"I would think you'd be used to this style of home since you were once in Jedediah's house." The queen pointed to a loveseat. "Please have a seat. Elsie, inform the kitchens we have guests."

The purple-haired vampire disappeared.

I latched onto Alex and limped toward the loveseat. "I wasn't allowed into Jed's house. The only time I saw him was when he needed a punching bag. He kept me in a shack." I figured I might get out of the mess if I was blunt and honest.

Both ancient vampires ramped up their magic. I closed my eyes and soaked it in because it felt so good. When I opened them, I saw goosebumps rise on Powerhouse's arms.

Perfect Suit recovered first. "May we call you Liliana?"

"I hate that name. You can call me Lily." My muscles relaxed as his magic wrapped around me. It felt like a gentle hug or coming home. "Your magic feels amazing."

The Vampire Queen's face lit up. "Thank you, dear. I am Ara, and this gentleman is my consort, Tarquin. You may call me Meemaw."

She wanted me to call her the southern term for grandma? I made a strangled sound. "Okay." I waved a hand toward Tarquin. "Should I call him Papaw or Gramps?"

His eyes narrowed. He did not like that. "You may call me—"

"Gramps is perfect!" Meemaw clasped her hands in front of her.

The man's lips twisted in disgust.

I almost burst out laughing. At least I could have a little fun before they killed me.

Alex elbowed me in the ribs. "Stop it."

I turned my attention to Powerhouse. Her face remained neutral, but her eyes sparkled with humor. "You can call me Jenella or Jen. Either's fine."

I motioned to Alex. "This is my adopted brother, Alex."

A vampire zipped in and set glasses of punch or tea in front of each of us and was gone in a heartbeat. By the extra glass, I assumed they were expecting company.

My hand shook as I picked mine up and took a sip. The sweet nectar hit my tastebuds, and it was all I could do not to moan. "Wow. That's delicious." I wondered if they would think less of me if I chugged it.

Alex took a sip of his and shrugged.

The doors to the room opened, and the hairs on the back of my neck rose as the Bloody Prince strode in. He scanned the room as he made his way toward us. The confidence continued to amaze me. It was a type of energy that was hard to comprehend until you saw it. Like he knew he was the biggest badass in the room and didn't need to prove it. Which was saying a lot, considering the current company. He inclined his head toward the vampires and owned, rather than sat in, the chair next to Jen. His golden eyes assessed me. "Lily. It's good to see you again."

I focused on the best tea I'd ever had. "Hello, Prince Mathias. Sorry about all of this."

"Wait. You two know each other?" Jen's voice was a tad bitter.

He ignored her disdain. "We met a couple of weeks ago when the palace guards misread her magic as Bellicose. She's the adopted daughter of Jonas the First and an honorary member of the House of Roman."

The room went silent for a few heartbeats. My mouth went dry, and I crossed my legs to stop myself from bolting out the door.

Ara crossed her legs at the same time. "Interesting. Tell me, Lily, how did that come to be?"

"Which part? Because both stories are long and complicated."

"Start from the beginning."

I rubbed my face. "I spent the first twelve years of my life on the run with my biological mother. In hindsight, she was an awful person. I didn't know it at the time because when you're a kid, you don't know what's normal. She was a mage who insisted on shoving supernatural politics and laws down my throat." I pointed at Jen. "I think she was trying to turn me into you, though it took years of therapy for me to realize that."

Jen's eyes sparked with something I couldn't read.

I held up a hand before she could comment. "We'd move every few weeks because she claimed people were chasing her, though I never saw nor sensed anyone. We stayed in slums, but she carried herself as if she was better than everyone else. Other people never appreciated that. It was not a good time. Around the time I turned twelve, she dumped me off with good old Jed."

The prince leaned forward. "On your twelfth birthday?"

I shrugged. "I don't know when my birthday is."

He rubbed his chin and leaned back. "Go on."

"Right. My time with Jed was also a barrel of laughs. As soon as she left, he backhanded me and called me an abomination. Then made it clear I wasn't welcome inside his house. I got locked in a shack at the back of his property, and he kept me filthy and starved. Eventually, his security took pity on me and brought me supplies. I'm pretty sure they're all dead now." I stared at my drink and waited for the tightness in my chest to ease. After years of my parent's love combined with therapy, I had some pretty good coping strategies.

"One night, a few of his vampires attacked me. By the scent of anticipation rolling off those assholes, I knew what they were after. I'll skip the details, but I panicked. My bio mother instilled fear in me about using my magic. But if I don't use it, then it builds until it explodes." I met Jen's eyes, who had somewhat similar magic to me. But she didn't look like she recognized the feeling.

Reminding myself I was almost done with the story, I took a shaky breath. "I let it explode to save myself and ran like hell. A lone wolf found me just outside the gates of Allure. I was bloody, my clothes torn, and a little feral. He took me to Jonas and Ann Marie."

I picked at a thread on my torn jeans. "They took me in, got me psychological help, gave me the best brother in the world, and taught us everything they could." I took another gulp of air. "Roman rejected me when I went to him for help shortly after the adoption. When the purebloods started following Alex, I approached him again, and he agreed to negotiate. He even tried to teach me more about my vampire skills. We became allies, and he made me an honorary house member. He thought I'd have less trouble in Allure if I belonged to a house. It didn't work."

Silence filled the room, and I didn't dare meet anyone's eyes. "And that's the story of Lily."

Jen shifted in her chair, and I raised my head. Her eyes were watering. I hated it when people felt sorry for me, so I focused on Mathias.

He examined me with his usual air of confidence, his face a stony mask. "Tell me more about your biological mother."

"You'd know more about her than me. I once asked her why she ran away from others if she was so important. She went on a tirade about how useless children were and told me she'd make sure I was the exception." I shivered. "That woman didn't love or have any empathy. She told people what to do and expected them to follow her orders." I closed my eyes, trying to picture her. Thanks to my vampire brain, I had a great memory, but I compartmentalized and forgot things from my childhood to protect myself. I met Mat's eyes. Unexpected emotions swirled in them, but I didn't know him well enough to read them. "I can't think of anything right now."

Ara patted my arm. "It's okay, dear. We will move along. What has Roman told you about your vampire heritage?"

"That I don't have one. He thinks Jed turned me when I was a baby, and my mage abilities developed over the vampire virus."

Tarquin leaned forward. "Show me your fangs."

I flipped my fangs out and opened my mouth enough for them to see.

He leaned back and rubbed his chin. "Interesting."

I retracted the fangs. "Not much of a conversationalist, eh, Gramps?"

"No."

The interrogation was interrupted when Purple Hair led two mages into the room. They didn't hide their shaking as they bowed toward Jen. "Your Grace." Then, toward Ara. "Mistress. What can we do for you?"

Ara squared her shoulders. "I want you to test this woman's magic patterns and DNA against ours."

Jen raised her hand like she was in school, caught herself, and lowered it. "Test her against us, too."

Alex elbowed me when I opened my mouth to protest. Then the little snot sent pictures of torture chambers into my head. I rubbed my temples to clear it. "I already know we share a mother. She made a big deal about how awful you were and how I needed to replace you." I held up a hand. "Which isn't something I'd do. I just want to go home, save people, and find a new toxic workplace."

A kind smile formed on Jen's face. "Let's get the tests, then we can talk about Anitta's plans."

"She's dead," the bloody prince said. "She was the one responsible for the damage to the castle and Dragon Headquarters."

For a split second, I thought about acting surprised. But I felt nothing but visceral hatred toward her. I didn't owe that bitch anything. "Good. I'll tick that task off my list."

His eyes bore into me. "You hate her as much as I do, then."

"Everyone smart enough to see past her public persona hates her." I eyed the wide-eyed mages who still stood with Elsie. "Those guys gonna be a problem?"

When Ara laughed, it sounded like a small bell ringing. "No, dear. They're under contract."

"Great. Let's get this over with. I have things to do."

After the mages took blood, magic, and hair samples, we moved to a covered back patio with a swimming pool, sauna, and jacuzzi. I gazed longingly at the back wall of the property, where I could just see a hazy outline of the turret on top of Cavil's house. My stomach was in knots, and I wrestled with the urge to run for the property line and beg Cavil for help. I shook off the thought and turned to Jen. "Why is your magic ballooning out of control?"

She frowned. "I don't know what you mean."

I was great at gauging the amount of power a person had. Mages, including Mathias, usually absorbed and held magic rather than creating it. Jen's wasn't as dark as mine, but I could feel her generating it like I did. Hers felt a lot like my mother's, only on steroids.

I pointed to her chest. "You should probably release some before it explodes. I took out a good chunk of Jed's property when I let mine build up, and you're far more powerful than me. You could take out the whole pocket."

Jen's eyes widened, and she snapped her head to Mathias.

He shook his head.

"Ah. So you don't know how." I turned my attention to the vampires. "How long will this take? Because Alex and I will be going home. I don't want to be anywhere near this wretched pocket when she explodes."

Jen hopped out of her chair. "Wait. You know how to use this magic?"

"Yeah. My magic is different. Darker. But if yours is anything like the bitch that birthed us, it's the same basic technique."

"Show me."

My nerves were fried, and I needed something to do, so I dragged her into the center of the back lawn. "This is how mother guided me. Keep in mind that my magic is dark. It manifests dark, bloody things. Yours is cleaner and you have a lot more."

"Got it."

I latched on to her magic. The sting of her intense, clean power almost knocked me off my feet. "Wow. You pack a punch. Pay attention to how I do this."

I formed a small wall the size of a door in front of us, careful not to aim it at anyone. After I tied the anchor to keep it in place, I let her magic go and dropped her hand. It looked like a normal wall, and for a few seconds, I wondered if it was going to stay that way.

Twelve-inch arrows exploded from it and lodged themselves toward the back wall. A spray of something coated the grass underneath. It withered and died. The vampires on the wall looked on with mixed expressions of shock and horror.

I waved an arm. "Sorry!" I turned my attention back to Jen. "The bloody poisoned spikes are the part you shouldn't have, in case you were wondering."

The disgust I expected to see was absent. Instead, she tilted her head as a blinding smile lit her face. "I like the bloody spikes. They're you."

I chuckled. "Give it a try."

She formed a solid wall, anchored it, and released it. No bloody spikes. Then she did a couple more for good measure, a huge smile on her face the whole time. "That's really easy."

"Yeah." My eyes swept over her. This woman was supposed to be our new hope. The one to staunch the rebellion. And she couldn't even do basic magic? The hope I had for getting out of our current situation withered and died. I wondered if Mom and Dad would move to Europe with us. "No offense, but how in the hell do you plan to keep the coalition together when you can't even use your magic?"

A plethora of emotions darted across her face. "When I was a kid, assassins chased us for almost a year. I learned how to hide my magic, but screwed it up in the process. It's fixed now, but different."

I rubbed my face. "You're supposed to be the one who swoops in and saves us. The new queen to unite and rule us all. The chosen one. Yet you have no confidence." I leaned in. "What are you so passionate about that you will kill or die for?" I jerked a thumb toward Alex. "For me, it's my adopted family and the hybrids. But I don't sense that you give a shit about much. Because if you did, you would have figured this out by now."

"Hey! I have things," she screeched. Mathias stomped toward us, and she threw a wall in front of him. "Stay out of this, Mat."

I folded my arms and stared at her magic, thinking. "Okay. You're a quick study and have a buttload of magic. I'll show you the three...no, four things that I do to release mine. You need to practice them until the pressure in your chest eases. Preferably before you explode. I have a friend who can help teach you more. It's up to you to decide if you give a shit enough to learn."

"I told you I give a shit. Am I conflicted? Yes. But I'm figuring it out." She started pacing. "I've been doing magic my whole life, so I'm sure I can learn it fast. But here's the thing. You can't tell anyone about my...shortcomings. Very few people know, and I can't have it getting out."

"I can keep a secret. And I'll help you because it's what my family does. We rescue people. Though, I've never met someone who needed rescuing from herself before." I said that part to get under her skin. "Besides, if someone doesn't do something, we're all screwed."

Her face grew serious. "I am aware. Who is your friend?"

I grinned. "Cavil." I pointed to the back wall. "He's a god. He said the First Drake already asked him to help you."

Her eyes widened. "He showed up in the battle for a minute to help, but I haven't seen him since."

"I'll give you his number." I showed her how to create with her magic. Then I watched as she not only made her own perfect boxes, spears, walls, and spells. She even mimicked the carnage my magic created. Just like my mother used to do. It was surreal. Though Jen wasn't anything like that bitch. She had emotions and empathy. I found it hard not to like her as we practiced.

The mages killed the vibe when they stepped out the back door. My shoulders slumped as I tiptoed over and lowered myself into a chair.

The female mage clasped her hands behind her back. "I've confirmed that Liliana First is the biological granddaughter of Mistress Ara and Consort Tarquin. She is a full sister to her grace, Jenella, and two-thirds sister to his majesty, Mathias. Liliana's magic is unique. She is a high-level mage of Ahl, with a touch of the ruling magic of Lissa."

"Ruling magic?" Jen asked.

The mage nodded. "Only a touch. Her levels are on par with Prince Mathias's. She is also a natural-born vampire. However, she's much more powerful than Master Jedediah or Mistress Vesna, considering her age. We've determined her power boost comes from ruling magic consistent with Lilith's bloodline."

"Unique indeed." The glee in Ara's voice made my skin crawl.

The mage nodded. "As with all hybrids, these magics have blended. Liliana is the most unique one I have ever tested."

"What do you mean by blended?" Jen asked.

"Many paranormals have a recent belief that hybrids are weaker than those with a single magic type. But that is incorrect. It is often the opposite. They inherit a full dose of both magics. For example, if a shifter and a witch have a child, fate grants that child the full ability to weave spells and shift. As they grow, those magics blend and form a unique and powerful type of magic. It is rare to find a low, or even mid-powered, hybrid."

"How can I be a two-thirds sister?" My voice quivered a little because my mind was spinning. The whole analysis terrified me, even though Mom and I talked about it at length. Back then, it was a theory. Having the reality slap me in the face was a whole different experience.

"I have only seen it twice over my long life. It is always when one parent is a possessor. Possessors can merge their bodies with that of another. Our tests show Prince Mathias and Liliana First each have three biological parents. Liliana's parents include the second queen as one-half of her heritage, with the other half split between the Second Consort and Prince Jedediah. Prince Mathias's second father is an unknown mage. Queen Jenella has only two parents, the Second Queen and her consort. Magically speaking, the vampire virus and the magic of Lissa are both dominant. So, any gifts Liliana may have inherited from the consort are null, but the DNA is consistent. Prince Mathias inherited magic from all three parents."

I hyperventilated. When I bent over to put my head between my knees to breathe, my stomach revolted, so I sat back up and wheezed. Alex patted me on the back but didn't offer platitudes. I appreciated it. I swiped my sleeve across my face and froze. All eyes were on me. I went to the lawn and lost my lunch.

A soft hand settled on my shoulder. "It'll be okay, Lily. We'll figure this out." Jen's voice sounded as shaky as I felt.

"Sorry. This is lame." I straightened. "I always knew. But hearing it." I sucked in some air. "I had myself convinced that I could just live my life and not have to face any of this. Any of you. No offense. This whole situation sucks."

She handed me a potion. "This will clean out your mouth and make you feel better. My friend Tracy is an excellent alchemist, so it's safe."

I took the potion, opened the bottle, and downed the contents. I didn't care if it killed me. "Is that the gorgeous witch that was with you?"

"Yeah."

CHAPTER SIXTEEN

THE MAGES WERE GONE when I returned to the group. "So, where does that leave us?" I motioned between me and Alex. "Because Alex is still my brother, and Jonas and Ann Marie are still my parents, and you can't change that. I refuse to be something I'm not and won't be moving to Allure."

The statement was directed at Ara, but Mathias dropped the next bombshell on me. "You are both a princess of Ahl and Umbra. You will be treated as such."

"Oh, hell no."

Alex slapped a hand on my arm. "Lily needs time to process and we need to talk to our parents. I'd like to take her back to the hotel now, if you don't mind."

Ara stood. "Of course, dear. I'll just send Elsie with you."

I rubbed my temples. The last thing I needed was more vampires hanging around. "No. I don't need more vampire spies in my life."

"The dragons probably won't like one hanging around," Alex added.

Tarquin, or Quin, as Jen called him, appeared a couple of inches from my face.

I jumped back. For a split second, I thought letting us go might be a ruse. "Dude. Ever heard of personal space?"

"What vampire spies?"

I'd long since boarded the crazy train, so I spilled my guts. I told them everything Jed had done in the last few months, including how Roman kept picking off the members of his house. "Didn't you get those two vampires who stowed away in my van? I thought the gate guards were going to bring them here." The temperature dropped and the vampire magic became so thick I had to focus on breathing. I rubbed my arms. "Oh, and he sent me an invitation to have dinner here."

Ara's eyes glowed. "I did not expect Jedediah to cause you such grief when I made my demands that he present you to me. He will be punished for that. And, yes, we have the vampires. They are staying here until they choose another house."

I shook my head. "They need to stay with you or go to Roman. If they go to a weaker House Master, Jed will kill them."

"Of course, dear." I didn't realize she'd moved until her arm linked with mine. "Don't worry about them. They will find a suitable house where they will be safe. Now, let's blood bond Elsie to you so she cannot spy."

"I'd rather not." I rubbed my stomach with my free hand.

Ara dragged me into a small office, Elsie trailing behind. By her sour expression, she wasn't any happier about it than me. Before I could register that thought, my palm had a gash in it. Elsie licked it and said some words in a language I didn't speak. Then her palm got shoved in my face.

I had two choices. Either fight the blood bond or take the badass woman with me and let the dragons deal with her. I needed to get out of there and think, so I licked the blood. And tried not to barf. Ara was unaware that I didn't need it, and I wasn't going to tell her. She might force-feed it to me and pretend it's for my own good.

A tingle formed in my middle, and I doubled over. "Can this day get any shittier?" I mumbled as it spread through my body. When her intentions flooded my brain, I threw them into the back of my head.

A tinkling laugh filled the kitchen. "You are an amazing creature. It took me nearly a year to mute my first blood bond."

I blinked.

"It's fine, dear. Elsie is very old and not inclined to cause trouble." Ara led us toward the front door.

"Then she's in the wrong house. You should take her back now before I get her killed."

Another tinkering laugh. "Don't be ridiculous. She will help you protect Alex."

She played on my protective instincts to manipulate me. I glanced at Elsie, then shook my head. "I don't think this is a good idea, Meemaw."

Ara's face grew serious. "I, too, have protective instincts. And they are telling me to keep you here and never let you out of my sight again. Elsie is a compromise." She leaned forward. "I do not want the knowledge of your vampire heritage to get out until after the family dinner on Friday. I wish to see what Jedediah has planned for you. But I do so want a relationship. I will enjoy getting to know you and your wonderful brother."

Daylight peeked through the front door, and I fought the urge to run for it. "Okay. I'll take Elsie with me to help settle your instincts. But I will not be held responsible if the dragons eat her."

Ara's face lit up, and I found myself wrapped in a hug. I patted her back awkwardly.

She stepped back and squeezed my hand. "I will see you tomorrow for lunch."

It was an order, but I didn't argue. Instead, I grabbed Alex's arm and made a beeline out the door and through the gates. Elsie followed, her intelligent eyes scanning the area.

Jen and Mathias waited for us inside the nearby flashing circle. My shoulders slumped. "Please tell me you aren't waiting for us."

"We're waiting for you." Mathias put a hand on Jen's arm and reached toward me with the other. "You're flashing to the main square, correct?"

Alex stepped in front of me to block him. "I'll take Lily and Elsie."

Mathias's face grew hard. "I will not harm Lily."

"I don't care." Alex slapped his hands on us and bright light exploded before the beautiful buildings surrounding the square appeared.

I didn't speak as we made our way out of the circle. Mathias and Jen somehow ended up in front of us, so we followed them through the narrow cobblestone streets toward the hotel. Several people stopped and stared at them. Some even bowed. I watched with an interest normally reserved for mid-level managers who liked to throw their power around in the workplace. It was fascinating how they ignored it. Like the people bowing were beneath them somehow. I guessed they were.

The yellow dragon stood at the entrance to the hotel and bowed. I didn't have the heart to tell him the gesture was wasted on the two royals. "Your Grace. Welcome to our establishment." He eyed us. "Have the hybrids caused trouble?"

Jen snorted in a very non-royal way. "I doubt Lily's stayed out of trouble a day in her life. Is Glacintial around?"

He opened the door and patted me on the shoulder in solidarity. "He is manning the front desk."

Jen shoved Mathias out of the way and linked arms with me. "The dragons like you."

"It's mutual. They're an amazing species who can really hold their liquor. I had to forfeit the drinking game, which was a first for me."

She blinked. "Wow. You can drink with dragons. Interesting."

"You should try it sometime. It's a little dangerous when the fire-blowing contests start, but otherwise, loads of fun."

"Jenella will not be drinking with dragons," Mathias interjected.

I jerked a thumb over my shoulder. "He's a real barrel of laughs, eh?"

She winked.

The white dragon, Glacintial, who checked us in that first night, rested his elbows on the counter. The guy was fun when you got a few shots of tequila in him. His white eyes focused on me with zero emotion. "What kind of shit have you stepped in, Lily?"

I sighed.

Mathias stepped in front of me. "Don't talk to her like that."

I went fluid and appeared in front of him. "Apparently, I'm related to these two. I have to tell you, Glac, I'm not thrilled with the idea." I leaned forward and fake whispered, "the prince is kind of a wet blanket."

Glac threw his head back and laughed. "I adore you, Lily. I'll be sad if I must eat you."

Jen threw a hand up. "No one is eating anyone. Lily isn't causing trouble. I wanted to make sure she and Alex were okay here."

Glac stretched to his full height. I had to crane my neck to see his face. "I am insulted by the insinuation that I would mistreat Lily and Alex, who are not only model guests but have breathed new life into my establishment."

"She didn't mean that." Alex used his calm and reasonable voice. "The queen just learned she has a sister and wants to make sure she's okay. I told her we were welcomed with open arms here, but she wanted to see for herself. She trusts the dragons because of her match."

"Stay out of my head, Alex," Jen said. "He's right, though. I want Lily to know she has support and protection here."

Glac bared his teeth in what I assumed was a smile. "Protection? You do not know Lily very well." He pointed at me. "That vampire can hold her own drinking with dragons. Besides that lovely character trait, those two hybrids are a force of nature. I am surprised you have not heard of their recent exploits."

Alex nodded. "Our parents didn't send us here because we couldn't take care of ourselves."

I jerked my thumb toward Elsie. "The Vampire Queen bonded Elsie to me. Is it cool if she stays in my room? I'll pay extra."

"Can she drink?"

I turned to Elsie and raised an eyebrow.

"My job is to protect Mistress Lily. I won't let my guard down by playing drinking games with dragons."

"Pity. You have no idea the fun you're missing." I turned back to Jen. "We good here?"

The five of us piled into the elevator. Mathias body-blocked Jen from both the door and us. I opened my mouth to say something, only to have Alex's hand cover it. "No."

I dropped my head to my toes. "I was only going to say that they have a weird dynamic."

"Shut up, Lily."

"Honestly, Alex. I only wondered if Prince Wet Blanket used his magic to suck all of Jen's confidence and keep it for himself. Because you'd think their demeanors would either be equal or she'd have the most. You know, being queen and all."

He face-palmed. "Just stop."

"What? I'm only saying that it's weird how Mathias is way too over-confident, where Jen lacks it. Not even Dad or Drake have that much confidence, and they're older than dirt."

Jen's spine straightened. "You know Drake?"

"Not really, no. He was at our parents' house the other day. I used him as an example to emphasize the overconfidence."

Alex cleared his throat.

The prince's eyes twinkled, although his hard expression didn't change. "I carry myself that way because it tells would-be enemies I am not concerned about winning should they attack. I imagine it is as effective as your smack talk and snark. You can call me Mat. It is much easier to say than Prince Wet Blanket."

My desire to chip away at his confidence melted. I held up a peace sign. "Respect."

Mat and Jen didn't stay long, and Alex fell asleep halfway through the long, uncomfortable conversation with our parents. Mom said she knew I'd run into them if I stayed in Allure. She confirmed that she had arranged for the dragons to take us in. I wasn't sure how I felt about that. Especially since she'd worked overtime to hide me from the royals for so many years.

Dad said the situation was more dangerous than we knew. He believed we were safer with my biological family, but knew I'd never meet them voluntarily, so Mom asked Jen for help. He liked her and thought she'd treat us well. They also thought Ara would protect me from Jed.

They cautioned us to be careful, but encouraged me to give them a chance. I threw up a couple of more times and brushed my teeth the old-fashioned way.

I tried to find things I liked about the pocket as I strolled through the downtown area, thinking. Dragons, griffins, fairies, pixies, and other flying paranormals filled the sky, going about their business without a care in the world. Shifters walked around naked or in their animal form. A mage juggled a ball of bright white magic as he waited near the main flashing circles. I tried to track the bright streak of a vampire wearing a red dress. She stopped in front of an ogre outside of a restaurant, shared a few words with him, and they both threw their heads back and laughed.

I liked how everyone could be themselves and wondered how different it would be if hybrids were included. Probably not much, I decided.

The stabbing in my chest indicating familial bonds came from three directions, and I stopped on the street to consider each one. The one that felt like Mat was in the direction of the castle. My new grandparents were close to him, probably at their house. So the other one was Jen's, and it was across the city.

Cavil appeared in one of the circles. He scanned the area, his eyes landing on me. He looked like he stepped out of a fashion magazine or a professional wrestling match as he strolled toward me.

"It should be illegal to look that good," I blurted when he got within hearing distance.

He grinned. "Hello, Lily."

"Hey. What are you doing here?"

He motioned toward one of the nearby streets. "Come. I'll show you a spot I found."

"Sure." I started in the direction he pointed. "I forgot to ask you, how do you like your new house?"

"It's perfect. I have reconsidered the receiving room's décor."

"Sorry about that. I shouldn't have said anything."

Cavil guided me to a nearby park and toward a gazebo. "I like this park. I often come here to clear my head." His eyes swept over my face. "What's wrong, Lily?"

The story came gushing out of my mouth before my brain engaged. I told him everything, using my sleeve to wipe away tears as they leaked out of my eyes. "They'll try to make me something I'm not. I like my life. I enjoy saving foul-mouthed gnomes and gods that don't really need my help. Working human jobs and drinking at Dale's bar are just fine with me. I hate Allure and the stupid way they treat hybrids. Except for the dragons. They're great." Realizing I'd over shared, I shut my mouth with a click.

When I met his eyes, the concern in them was so deep that I almost ran away. He ran a thumb across my cheek to wipe away a tear. His arms came around me, and he pulled me to his chest.

I couldn't help myself. I curled into him and let the tears flow. It was an ugly cry and more than a little embarrassing. After I soaked up his warmth, I pulled back and swiped my sleeve over my eyes. "I can't believe you let me cry and slobber all over your white dress shirt."

"I'm not worried about my shirt. My concern is for you. Family can be...difficult."

There was a story there. I was sure of it. "You too, eh?"

"My parents chose death when I was a child. My eldest sister placed me in servitude. I escaped when I came of age, and they have since disowned me."

"I'm sorry. That's awful."

He nodded. "It was. Until I built a following based on compassion and became more powerful than them. Now, they are nothing to me."

I doubted that, but didn't want to pry. "Sorry about this. I didn't mean to come here and dump on you. I'll get you a new shirt."

He created a handkerchief, handed it to me, and turned his attention to the entrance to the park. "The vampire lurking in the shadows is yours?"

"Yeah. That's Elsie. She's a badass." I had a sudden urge to run away as fast as I could. What kind of idiot dumps such heavy problems on someone she barely knows and then pries into their past? I stood. "Sorry. I don't know what came over me just then. Can you forget I said any of that?"

"No." He yanked me back down. "I also won't forget that you gave the queen my phone number to assist in her training. That was kind of you to help me establish a powerful connection."

"Except you already agreed to help her." I shook my head. "I did it for her. Jen's my next rescue, and I thought you could help."

He rubbed his chin. "It doesn't matter. The First Drake didn't give me her phone number. It makes training easier." He dropped his hand. "I don't fully understand families in this realm. I do know that you are not the kind of person to let anyone push you around, no matter how powerful. If you want to keep your life in the human world, you will. And I will stand by your side, as will Alex and your parents."

"That's just it. I kind of want to get to know them. And that's terrifying, considering my history and their titles. But Jen's quirky and cool. Mat's stoic, which makes him super fun to mess with. And my grandparents... Well, I don't know what to think about them, but they're nothing like Jed. I don't know what to do."

Cavil's eyes lost their sparkle. "No one said you need to make life-altering decisions today. If your biological family does not give you time to adjust or understand how difficult this is, then they do not deserve you. Your time here in Allure is a chance to get to know them, so use it. And if you need to escape, you know where to find me. Perhaps I can return the favor of rescuing someone who does not need rescuing."

A smile touched my lips. "Perhaps." I stood. "I really should get going before Elsie tries to rescue me." We strolled toward the park's entrance. "So, when are you going to help Jen? Because she's in deep shit."

"In the morning at the dragon tower. Will you come with me?"

I almost rejected the idea. But it gave me a chance to get to know her better, and with Cavil and his unwanted oath there, no one would mess with me. "Sure. If the dragons and palace guards will let me and my entourage in."

He nodded. "Showing up unexpectedly is a good way to gauge their acceptance of you."

We stopped near Elsie. "I doubt Jen will have a problem with it. Mat might, but he won't make a public spectacle."

Cavil swiped a stray curl out of my face, and I felt his sunshine magic wash over me. I closed my eyes to savor the warm, welcoming feeling. Amusement danced in his eyes when I opened them. "Then I'll meet you in front of the dragon palace at six."

He inclined his head toward Elsie. "Good night, Lily."

"Night, Cavil."

Elsie didn't say anything as we made our way toward the hotel. Traveling with someone who could move as fast as me was fun. I headed straight for the bar. If I wanted to go with Cavil in the morning, I couldn't drink, but I didn't want to sit in the hotel room. I ordered water, and Elsie ordered a soda.

She turned her hard face toward me. "You left without me."

"Good deduction, Watson." When she didn't respond, I let out a breath. "It's been quite a day. I needed to take a walk and ran into a friend."

"You and Alex are being followed by an organization with a lot of resources. I'm supposed to have your back. If you leave me behind and something happens to you, I'll lose the status I've spent years working on and receive a harsh punishment. The status I can live without, but I don't like torture. Don't do it again."

I blinked. "Is Meemaw that bad?"

"She expects a certain standard of conduct from her elite vampires. Allowing her granddaughter to die because she's stubborn violates those standards."

"Yikes. I guess you told me."

A man with red hair and eyes slid onto the barstool beside me. "Not drinking tonight, Lily?"

"Hey, Flintous. Nope. My new buddy and I are letting Alex sleep."

His red eyes examined Elsie. "Since when are you friendly with vampires?"

"Since their queen said so."

He grinned. "Does Ara think we are incapable of protecting you?"

"I don't want to know what she thinks. Unless, of course, you're trying to rile Elsie. Then I need to warn you it's a bad idea. She almost beat me in a fight today."

He frowned. "I heard about a disturbance near the House of Umbra. I should have known it was you. Vampires have no tolerance for intruders in their territory."

"Yeah, I got that." I sipped my water.

"Why is the Vampire Queen meddling in your affairs?"

"Don't ask questions you don't want the answer to," I warned.

"Lily's her granddaughter," Elsie said.

"Well, I'll be damned. I should have guessed, considering your power level." He stood. "Hey, everyone! Lily's royalty!"

The entire bar burst out laughing. A giant man with lime green hair and eyes patted me on the back a little too hard. "Bullshit. Royalty doesn't hang out with grunts like us drinking and swearing."

I pointed at him. "Exactly."

Elsie stood. "They're right. You have no business drinking in a hotel bar."

I yanked her back down. "See, that's the thing, Elsie. This *is* my kind of environment. I'm a thousand times more comfortable here than at the vampire house."

She eyed me for a long moment. "Alright. But your grandparents will not like this."

"Tough shit." I winced at how harsh that sounded. "I gave up trying to meet other people's expectations a long time ago. If they don't like me for who I am, then that will suck, but I'm not changing to please them."

Respect and uncertainty flashed across her face before a genuine smile took over. "This assignment is going to be a wild ride."

Chapter Seventeen

The dragons who had culinary magic took great pleasure in showing it off. Alex and I sampled everything they'd thrown at us with delight. They glowed with pride when we liked their food, and each meal tasted better than the previous one.

The pink dragon at the coffee shop was no exception. When I told him where we were headed, he loaded us up with different flavors of coffee. As a result, the three of us each carried two trays when we met Cavil outside of Dragon Headquarters. I shoved a vanilla caramel something something in his hands.

"Thank you." His usual sunny disposition was absent.

I ignored the familial stabbing in my chest coming from two directions and the tingle between my shoulder blades from being watched as I tilted my head toward the drink. "Coffee made by culinary magic. Why do you look so serious?"

He squinted at the cup. "Because you failed to mention my superior good looks."

I couldn't help the laugh that escaped as I tried to ignore the butterflies erupting in my stomach. "It's no fun if you're expecting it."

Cavil's eyes sparkled with humor. "Come. Let's see if we can help the queen."

"Why are you meeting her here instead of at the castle?" Alex asked.

Cavil took a tray from me and started up the stairs. "I don't know. A very pushy assistant insisted on the time and place. I did not know if it was possible to question the queen in this realm. In my realm, it is punishable by death."

Alex shuffled his trays of coffee around and held the door open. "I doubt that's the case here. The queen needs help, and your timing in coming to this realm is perfect. So perfect that I bet the prince questions it."

A stalky woman with deep purple hair and eyes examined us as we approached the security station. "Hey, Lily, Alex. What brings you here this morning?"

"What's up, June?" I set a coffee in front of her. I liked her. She could drink the male dragons under the table and was proud of it. "We're here with our friend, Cavil." I jerked my head in his direction. "He has an appointment with Queen Jenella."

It took a couple of minutes, but she let us through. Before I knew it, we were stepping into a huge gym-like thing. The ceilings were at least twenty feet high. Thick mats covered the floors. A line of chairs and a few long, skinny tables dotted the perimeter. One had a giant jug of water with a spout and paper cups. Jen, Mat, and a brunette I didn't know stood in front of it in a semi-circle. Their conversation died with our arrival.

I squared my shoulders and strode to the table to set the coffee tray down. "Hey, Jen, Mat. This is Cavil. The friend I told you about. Do you guys want coffee?"

Cavil bowed. "Your Grace."

Everyone ignored me and my coffee suggestion. Jen stepped forward. "Hello, Cavil. You can call me Jen or Jenella. Either's fine. And no bowing, please."

Mat cleared his throat. He didn't like Jen's informal greeting. I picked a couple of random coffees out of Elsie's tray and shoved one into his hand, then turned to the brunette. "I'm Lily. This is my brother, Alex, and my new buddy, Elsie. Do you want some coffee?" I held the cup out to her.

Her crazy blue eyes lit up. "I'm Emine. The sane one of the family. Oh boy. These two are not going to know what to do with you, are they?"

"No one ever does." I jiggled the cup.

She took it. "Hey, Jen. How long do you think it'll take you to get Lily into a stupid situation? I want to see what she's made of."

Jen rolled her eyes. "Stop it, Emine."

Alex grinned. He knew I didn't need any help with that. Apparently, Jen had the same personality quirk. Although, I couldn't imagine it based on her agreeable disposition.

A door opened, and a regal dragon with a ton of power strode in. Bastien, the guy who greeted us at the hotel that first night, followed behind. The gorgeous witch I'd seen at the vampire house by his side. Drake slipped in behind them and scanned the room. His eyes landed on Jen.

I drifted over to the chairs to watch the show. Alex sunk into a chair to my right while Elsie leaned against the wall behind us.

The bronze dragon stopped in front of Alex, blocking my view. They stared at each other long enough for a mind conversation. Her eyes sparkled with too much interest as she took the chair on his other side and patted his hand. "I'm thrilled to meet you. The hotel staff tells me you're wonderful guests."

"I'm Lily, Alex's sister." I motioned toward the table. "Do you want some coffee?"

"You may call me Deva. That's a very generous offer, love. What kind is it?"

I went to the table, picked one out, and handed it to her. "If you don't like this one, there's a bunch of different flavors. They're made by the coffee dragon at the hotel, so they're all good."

"This will be fine. Thank you."

Drake put an arm around Jen's shoulders and kissed her temple before moving to a chair on the other side of the room. Jen grabbed a coffee and sat beside me. The witch and Bastien took positions behind us against the wall with Elsie.

I turned to Jen and tried to hide my anticipation. "So, you and Drake, eh?"

Her eyes lit up. "Yes. We're newly bonded, but it's been building for a while. He's amazing."

I pretended to turn my attention to Cavil and watched her out of the corner of my eye. Just as she took a drink of coffee, I said, "I never thought I'd get to say my sister's banging my dad's oldest friend. Nice."

Coffee spewed from her mouth, and she coughed. I patted her back.

The witch threw a spell that slid off me and cleaned up the mess.

Alex rolled his eyes. "Why do you always gotta do that?"

"What? It's true. Don't you find it hilarious?"

"Not really, no. And it's not your business."

The dragon behind us snorted. At least someone found my antics amusing.

Cavil's lips twitched as he fought a smile. "I would like to start with creation magic. Remember that it is only a small part of what you can do. It is also the one you have in common with Lily. I'd like you both to participate so you can learn from each other." He pulled us to the center of the room, demonstrated the same technique I'd always used, and held out a tennis ball. "Make this as realistic as possible."

Jen went first. Hers looked perfect on the first try. He showed us how to anchor a small object and then motioned for me to go. I concentrated, created a similar one, and held it out. When it turned blood red, I dissipated it before it could maim the nearby royalty.

Cavil rubbed his chin. "I still believe your intentions are the problem. Though your power stems from night magic, it should not do that unless you want it to. Let's try a plant."

A perfect peony in full bloom formed in front of Jen. Mine was a cactus-type thing with two-inch thorns and red flowers that oozed blood.

Emine leaned over my cactus. "That's way more handy than the smell-good thing Jen made."

I appreciated the support.

"Try to concentrate on intent, Lily. You're trying too hard to not hurt anyone, so your thoughts of how you imagine your magic will respond are incorporated into the results," Cavil explained. "Stop thinking your magic is dangerous."

That was easier said than done.

"Make a chair, and we'll move on to more complicated lessons."

Jen waved a hand and a deep purple chair with ornate wooden legs and arms appeared.

I closed my eyes and tried not to think about how I could wipe out two entire royal families if I made a mistake. I chose a bean-bag chair because it was the least lethal option. As I formed it, I thought about their soft, squishy feel. I made the color black and anchored it. My hands tingled, which usually meant something awful was about to happen.

"You might want to stand back," I told Drake, who leaned over to examine it.

He moved next to Jen. "I recognize that magic."

I held up a hand. "I don't want to know." When the chair was done, I took a couple of steps back. My shoulders slumped when it changed from black to blood red.

When nothing happened, I released a breath and turned to Cavil. "I'm slowing Jen's progress down. She needs to...."

Gurgle.

Blurp.

I swung back toward the beanbag. My stomach fell as the outer part changed. Blotches of gelatinous goo formed on the surface and spread as if bleeding. The thing jiggled, then rolled at a glacial pace toward me. I tried to dissipate it, but it wouldn't respond. "Uh, Cavil?"

He held out his hand. "I can't eliminate it."

"What do you mean, you can't eliminate it? This was your idea." It picked up speed. I shoved Jen into Drake. "Get her out of here."

She elbowed him in the stomach as his arms wrapped around her. "What the hell, Lily. I'm not helpless here."

She created a clear wall around the blob. It shot toward the wall, crushed it, and continued toward us.

Heart pounding, I grabbed Jen and Cavil and went fluid. The blob went fluid after us.

The witch jumped up and threw a spell, a wicked one that should have exploded the blob.

It ricocheted and hit the wall.

Jen and I tumbled one way while Cavil went the other.

"Sorry." The blob switched directions and went after the witch. Bastien picked her up and ran toward the other side of the room.

Elsie appeared at my side. "Fix this before you start a war."

Great. Just what I needed.

Emine took out a bow and arrow and fired at it. The arrow bounced off.

The blob went after her, but she flashed across the room and pulled a gun.

"This is as crazy as my magic used to be, but more deadly." Jen's voice held amusement. "How did you make that thing?"

I grabbed her hand and ran toward Alex, who had changed into his lion form and stalked the blob. "I was trying to think of something that wouldn't wipe out two royal families."

"Which is why I told you not to think that," Cavil said.

"Stop this madness and get behind me." The dragon queen's voice echoed through my bones. I latched onto Jen's arm, went fluid, and ducked behind the dragons. The three of them took deep breaths and blew. I yanked Jen to the floor and covered her as white-hot fire streamed toward the blob. I flung my hands over my head as the backlash of the heat came back at us. A burning pain shot over my back and down my arms.

When cool air touched my neck, I raised my head and sighed in relief. The blob was a pile of ash in the middle of the room.

"I'm out," I said between breaths. The thing had run us ragged. "I'm going to kill someone if we keep doing this." That's why we set up the warehouse. It was too dangerous to practice magic around other people. I raised a shaky hand, brushed a fried curl out of my eyes, and ignored the scent of burning hair.

Drake's glowing green eyes focused on me as he helped Jen off the floor. "Has Jonas seen your magic?"

"Yeah. Lots of times. Why?" I looked Jen over to make sure she was okay, then examined my scorched arms. The burns weren't too bad.

His eyes flicked to a very interested Dragon Queen before returning to me. "I am surprised Jonas has not recognized your power."

I held up a hand. "Nope."

Deva stepped forward. "Are you sure? It feels different."

"Because of the poor execution."

"Nope. We're not going there. I'm already on learning things about my origins overload. This training is about Jen. You know, the woman with so much pent-up magic she's about to explode?"

Drake's lips twitched. "Very well. I'll wait until you are more emotionally stable to discuss it with you."

"I'm not...it's not...never mind. The point is, Jen is good at creation magic, but she has a long way to go before she releases enough."

"Agreed." Cavil created clothes for Alex and handed them to him before turning back to Jen. "One facet of your magic is creation. As the ruling class, your other strength is to mimic magic. Conjure a small sample, please."

She complied, holding out a ball. Small, faded strands of a thousand different colors ran through the silvery mixture. I leaned forward to get a better look. A pronounced golden line ran through it, sparkling against a deep green one. A tiny, deep red line streaked by. The rest were so pale I had to squint to see them. "That is so cool."

Cavil rested a hand on my shoulder. "You have already absorbed magic from Drake and Lily." He pointed to the green and red lines. "And I suspect you have been mimicking Mathias's magic most of your life." He pointed at the thick gold line.

Jen's mouth fell open. "How is that possible?"

Cavil shook his head. "I don't know. The point is, you can assimilate any magic you come in contact with."

"How?"

"That is the question. How did you connect to Lily's magic?" He pointed to the deep red line.

Her eyebrows drew together. "I didn't. She connected with me."

"Do you remember how that felt?"

"Yes."

Cavil turned and pointed. "Try to use that feeling and connect to Elsie. Do not connect to any other hybrids, including your witch friend, until you know what you're doing. Hybrid magic is individualized and will not serve your immediate purpose."

"Tracy's not a hybrid."

"She is," Drake said. "She's not considered one by the haters because alchemy and spell weaving are both witch magics."

Jen's eye twitched. "Haters?" She turned her attention to me. "He's obsessed with human clichés."

I shrugged because I didn't get it. Everyone talked about haters.

"Every time you connect, the respective color will deepen," Cavil continued. "Once the color is vivid, you can mimic it. Elsie is a good start for vampires."

"So I can turn into a vampire or shift into a dragon?"

"I don't know how magic operates in this realm. I advise you to use caution until you understand your capabilities."

Jen took a shaky breath. "This is insane. Ready, Elsie?"

"Sure." Elsie's sharp intake of breath caused me to swing around to see if she was okay. She put her hand up, then heaved a sigh of relief.

Cavil watched with interest, then pointed out the black line running through Jen's magic. "You connected far too deep. You need a small sip rather than a gulp."

"How do you know this?" Mat asked.

"I have spent the last hundred years guarding a Crown Princess in my realm. Jen's magic is identical."

So that was the servitude he talked about. I had a million questions, but they could wait until later. "Right. So, I'll just get out of here so you can practice without killer blobs chasing you around." I turned to Alex. "I need to go see my new meemaw. You coming?"

"I'll stay here. Deva said she'd help me perfect my mental magic."

My eyes flipped to Mat.

He inclined his head. He'd watch Alex's back.

"Okay. But don't go anywhere alone."

Alex rolled his eyes. "Yes, Mother."

Chapter Eighteen

The tingle between my shoulder blades started again as I stepped out the door and started down the stairs outside. There wasn't a second I hadn't felt watched since entering the pocket. "I'm not sure what I think about that mimicking power."

Elsie's eyes swept over the street. "It is the same power the first queen had."

My biological mother didn't have that, at least when I was with her. But then, I was always more powerful than her. I wondered if it skipped her and went to Jen. Not that it was any of my business. "Were you alive when she was around?"

"No. Mistress Ara mentioned it."

As we started down the stairs, I scanned for the source of my tingles. The street was busy. A group of naked wolf shifters gathered around a hotdog stand on the cobblestone street as a swarm of pixies in their tiny form zoomed overhead, doing circles and zig-zags, creating a colorful rainbow effect. A troll stomped down the street in one direction while a centaur couple argued on the other side of the road. "This city's insane."

Elsie snorted. "You get used to it after a while."

The yellow dragon stood at the door to the hotel, facing front as always. I needed to learn his name. His pale-yellow eyes flicked to us before turning back. I followed his gaze to the corner where two men loitered, focused on the front door of dragon headquarters. They either didn't recognize me or didn't care if I was there. "Shit." I went fluid and stopped behind the troll.

"What do you have?" Elsie asked.

"A mage and a witch on the corner opposite the hotel."

"You recognize them?"

"They're the guys who followed Alex the day I got fired."

Elsie pointed to a small crevice between two buildings, just beyond the guys. I wasted no time going fluid and ducking into it. Elsie squeezed in beside me. We were close enough to hear, but couldn't see them. Since the dragons knew they were there, I didn't need to.

I pulled my phone out and texted Alex.

They found us.

Where are you?'

Just outside HQ. Spying now.

Queen is aware.

I breathed a sigh of relief and closed my eyes to tune into the mage and witch.

Elsie elbowed me. "I got the eavesdropping."

"I thought you worked for me?"

She gave me a flat look. "Until you can listen without closing your eyes, I'll do the eavesdropping."

"Gotcha."

My phone buzzed with a text from Mat. *Dragons sent to apprehend the spies. Do not kill.'*

Sure enough, two dragons swooped down from the sky, picked the guys up, and flew away. "Damn it. I wanted to find out more."

Elsie pulled my arm. "Come on. We'll talk to Mistress Ara about it. She's got spies everywhere and might know something."

We went fluid all the way to the gated neighborhood where the important people lived. As I caught my breath, Elsie chatted with the palace guards.

Two wolf shifters rounded the corner. I pointed. "Those guys were at the hotdog stand."

Elsie eyed me. "Why are you winded? We didn't go very far."

"I can't go fluid all willy-nilly where I live." I'd gotten comfortable and lazy. That had to change. "Those guys have witches, mages, and shifters working for them. Don't you find that odd?"

"Not with the way they recruit."

"By kidnapping?"

"And that nasty magic. From what I understand, the second queen started the movement. Master Tarquin and the First Drake think someone else runs it. We haven't found him yet."

"Huh." I watched the wolves slink behind a bush down the street. A griffin launched off the wall and pursued them. "Let's get out of here."

My palace guard buddies were on duty. The female mage checked my ID and pointed to the other end of the checkpoint. "Wait over there."

I crossed my arms and pretended to be put out. "I thought we moved beyond the harass the hybrid game."

A mischievous smile spread across her face. "I like you, Princess Lily."

I held up a finger. "No. No titles."

She threw her head back and laughed. "Sorry, no can do." She held up the results from my ID scan. "Here's your new identity, Mistress."

The ID came up purple, blue, and black, with symbols of the House of Umbra and the Crown of Ahl. "Damn it. No. I'm trying to fly under the radar here."

The guard nodded enthusiastically. "I know, Your Highness. That's why it's so funny." She deactivated the ID and shoved me toward the exit. "You may continue on, Princess."

"This is not okay."

Her laughter echoed down the street.

The welcome at the House of Umbra was much different from the day before. As we approached the gates, I kept my arms loose at my sides in case I needed to fight. They swung open, and a vampire zipped out of the house in a blur.

I jumped back into a crouch.

He stopped in front of us and put a hand over his heart. "My apologies for startling you, Mistress."

I wiped my sweaty palms on my singed jeans. I probably should have changed clothes. "Sure."

He led us through the modern house with tile floors and tasteful décor. I didn't remember much about the mansion from the day before because guards surrounded us, and I was sure I'd die. It was comfortable with a spicy, delicious scent, like one of those home décor stores. I liked it. I hated myself for liking it.

The vampire opened a door and motioned us in. Elsie melted away as I stepped inside. I took in the industrial kitchen with multiple stainless-steel countertops, huge commercial-grade appliances, and a sea of work-areas. The scent of simmering stew and freshly baked bread filled my nose, and my stomach growled.

At the very end, next to a serving island with a half-circle seating area, stood the Vampire Queen herself. She wore a deep orange dress that would have looked professional if not for the ruffled apron she wore over it. Her waist-length hair was piled on her head, and her face reflected pure bliss as she stirred a pot. "Hello, Lily. You're just in time for lunch."

"You cook lunch yourself?" I asked as I accepted a glass of tea from a fly-by vampire.

"Not always. But I needed the break today."

I took a seat near the middle of the bar. I wasn't much for small talk and fought to figure out what to say. "You like to cook?"

"Oh yes. Every vampire is required to find a hobby as an outlet to keep us sane. I find cooking rewarding." She put a tray of rolls in the oven. "Tell me, dear. What are you interested in?"

"I like to work in toxic workplaces and absorb human drama."

"Your grandfather has a similar obsession."

I watched her chop vegetables at vampire speed and wondered if I could do that without cutting off a finger. "You seem stressed." The words popped out of my mouth before I could stop them. "Er, I mean. How are you? It's gotta be tough finding out you have an abomination for a granddaughter."

Her knife stopped and her eyes flashed red. "You will not call yourself that again. I forbid it."

"Ah, man. I completely messed up your chi. I apologize. That's what Jed calls me, not how I think of myself."

"I will deal with my son." She went back to chopping. "Tarquin and I consider you a gift. We are thrilled to have found you."

An awkward silence followed.

I clasped my hands in my lap and tried not to wring them. "How are you adjusting to all of this? To be honest, it's thrown me off my game. I can't imagine how stressful it is for you."

She added the vegetables to the pot and refilled my delicious tea-punch drink. I couldn't decide which it was because it had the floral taste and color of herbal tea mixed with the sweet taste of punch. "I've learned over my many long years that family is a gift. Though you came into our lives in an unorthodox way, I am as grateful you are here. There will be an adjustment period, but it will work out in the end. I am confident of that." She shuffled toward the fridge and opened it. "Stress is a part of life and one of the many reasons I like to cook."

It made me nervous that she was so calm. Too calm. "If you ever need a vacation, you can stay at my house. It's peaceful when spies and potential kidnappers aren't hanging around."

A smile lit her face. "You would have me as your guest?"

I shook off the chills that ran down my spine. "Sure. Come on over any time you need to get away for a mental health break. Stay off the lawn, though. My gnome friend is a little prickly."

She was around the counter and hugging me before I could finish the sentence. "Thank you. No one besides Tarquin ever thinks of my well-being. I am honored."

My new meemaw was a hugger. I patted her on the back twice, making a mental note to practice reacting to stealth hugs, so I wasn't so awkward. I released her when the familial stabbing in my chest increased. "You're family. If there's one thing our parents instilled in us, it's that family takes care of each other."

She released me and was back around the counter in the blink of an eye. Gramps strolled into the room, eyed me, then appeared in a seat to my right. A drive-by drink, from what I assumed was the serving vampire, appeared in front of him.

"Hey, Gramps. How're you?"

"The Bellicose are after your brother. They have spies throughout downtown with orders to kill you and take him. It is not safe for you to stay with the dragons any longer."

My shoulders stiffened. "I disagree. The dragons are the safest place for us because they don't take sh...er...crap from anyone. They have protective instincts like ours. As a bonus, they're a lot of fun to drink with."

"Oh yes, because drunken parties are the current priority."

I chuckled at his sarcasm. I liked my gramps. He was the perfect kind of surly, and the magic he shed felt like a warm blanket in winter. "I'm glad we understand each other. Besides, rumor has it they're also after my new sister."

He eyed me without expression. "You are very stubborn."

"Yes."

Ara dished up three bowls from the pot, put them on saucers, and then served up a plate of freshly baked rolls. "Our granddaughter has invited us to stay at her home. Isn't that wonderful?"

"It is suspicious."

I took another sip from my drink. "I'm not up to anything. Meemaw needs a vacation. You don't have to visit if it bothers you."

His eyes flipped back and forth between us. "Very well. As soon as it is safe, we will visit."

Meemaw's face lit with excitement. "I cannot wait."

Quin's eyes softened a little with her enthusiasm. When they turned back to me, they were hard as stone. "Jen is bonded to a First and has gained the trust of the Dragon Queen. You and your brother have neither of those factors in your favor."

"I suppose that's true if you disregard our parents, one of which is also a First. Besides, Deva likes Alex's mental magic and the dragons like us both."

"You and your brother will stay here or in a guest suite at the palace when it opens tomorrow."

The order ignited my anger. I clenched my fists so tight my nails bit into my palms. "No offense, but that's not your call. Don't get me wrong, I'd like to get to know you and Meemaw. But based on my history with vampires, including the show yesterday, I don't trust you. The dragons are the only ones who've openly accepted us here, while everyone else has treated us like shit. We feel safest with them. If it becomes unsafe, I'll be glad to reconsider your offer."

"Let it go, my love." Ara's voice carried a warning that I interpreted as 'don't screw this up.'

By the time Elsie and I headed back downtown, my heart and head were tied in knots. Ara tried to get me to choose another vampire for added protection, but I'd declined. I would have declined Elsie if I wasn't so eager to get out of there the day before. I appreciated the gesture, though. They seemed to care. "Dang it. I really like them," I said, more to myself than Elsie.

"Forgive me, Mistress, but I don't understand why you wouldn't. They're your grandparents."

I shook my head. "Call me Lily. And I blame Jed. He's a total asshole. I always thought his attitude came from them."

"We *are* all assholes. It's kind of in the job description."

"True. But you and my grandparents are good assholes. Jed is..."

"No need to tell me. He's my maker."

I almost got whiplash when my head snapped toward her. "Does that mean he has influence over you?"

"I forget how little you know about your heritage. We only stick with our makers for the first twenty years. When we get a handle on our bloodlust, the blood bond can be transferred. Mistress Ara wants us to become strong and trapping us with our maker hinders our growth. Once we're stable, we're free to move on or stay, but it's our choice.

"In my case, I counted the days. Master Jedediah's house was cutthroat, brutal, and overly competitive. It took him five years to approve my request to transfer, even after I found a house that suited me better. He thought I should remain loyal to him and forced me to compete for the transfer. The competition was designed to eliminate me. I almost died, but I won."

"Joke's on him, eh?"

"Yes. He didn't realize my potential because, to him, I was just another cog in the wheel. It didn't surprise me when I heard your story. He's tested other young vampires that way."

"If that's the case, then failing that test was the luckiest day of my life." I couldn't imagine the monster I would have become if I stayed with him.

"Correct. Mistress Ara is good to her people and often takes in vampires who need help. She wanted you to bond with someone you didn't need to control. Although she can still monitor us at any time."

"She knew about me. I saw her at my favorite bar right before all hell broke loose." I reached deep to find my connection to her, but I didn't feel it. "A strong familial connection lets me know when she's near, but I don't feel the bond."

"No one feels her. She's just there."

I wasn't sure what I thought about that. I hated the idea that someone could monitor me any time they wanted. But I also admired how well Meemaw held herself together with all that responsibility. The train of thought was interrupted when dread washed over me. I scanned the nearby buildings. We were halfway between the palace and downtown. "Do you feel that?"

"No. What?"

I turned in a slow circle, trying to figure it out. When I couldn't, I latched on to Elsie's arm. "Come on. Let's get out of here."

We went fluid all the way back to the hotel.

I marched right up to Glac, who sat on a stool in the hotel's lobby, watching two dragons arguing in the seating area. "Glac. I think we found something."

I ignored the goosebumps that formed when his white eyes focused on me. "Oh?"

"It was just a feeling, but it might be worth checking out."

He leaned forward, somehow growing more intense. "Where?"

I gave him the location. "You might not find anything, but my instincts are never wrong."

He nodded. "I'll deploy a team."

CHAPTER NINETEEN

I WAS UNNERVED AND off my game when Alex and I landed near where I had that feeling. The emotional and mental overload made my mind spin and tied my stomach in knots.

Glac said they didn't find anything in the area the night before, but they'd continue to monitor it. On top of that, I kept running my conversation with Ara and Quin through my head. Along with scenarios where everyone would piss off, and I could return to my life.

Was it unrealistic? Yes. Did I care? No. But I couldn't help feeling like the very foundation of my life shifted in a direction I didn't want to go. I'd had enough of that when my biological mother was in the picture.

I was so lost in my thoughts that I almost missed the slight rustling from the street to our right. Elsie caught it and went fluid as a black wolf flew out, claws and teeth extended.

I ducked out of the way, spun, and landed in a crouch.

Elsie stabbed him in the side with her claws.

More swarmed us.

Alex shifted, and I felt his magic wash over me. Three wolves hit the ground, blood pouring out of their noses. Neat trick, that.

My claws and fangs popped out as I went fluid, kicked a wolf in the stomach, and raked my claws across the neck of another. The first wolf recovered and slammed into my side.

Pain shot down my leg when his teeth sunk into my hip. I landed at an awkward angle. "Shit!" I screeched as I bounced to my feet. He latched onto my arm, and I heard a sharp 'crack' seconds before I felt the pain. I ignored the burning wounds on my side and the throb from my now broken arm. I went fluid and stabbed the hell out of both attackers so fast they didn't know what happened.

Alex went for the throat of one and swiped another with his paw, then sat on one.

I spun in a slow circle, looking for another wolf to fight. Elsie wrestled with one of the two remaining wolves while the other circled.

Alex charged and pounced. He landed on the wolf's back, stretched his massive jaw, and bit into its neck.

Elsie took care of the other one at the same time.

We moved toward each other, so we stood back-to-back. My stomach was raw, something that never happened to vampires. I turned on my magic sight and gasped. "Don't move, Elsie. That nasty magic is all over us."

"I've taken the immunity potion, so I'm good."

I frowned. "The same one Mom fed to us?" I pulled out my phone, but I didn't get the chance to text anyone. Enforcers popped into existence around us. "You guys don't use the circles, eh?" I put my good arm under the broken one.

A hard-faced elf stepped forward. "What happened here?"

"Ummm. A fight? They lost."

Elsie elbowed my bad side. "We were attacked and defended ourselves."

He eyed the wolves. All but three were dead. "A single shifter and two vampires took out an entire pack of wolves?"

I checked the gash on my side. "You might want to have someone with magic sight take a look. There's some bad juju surrounding these guys."

The elf's eyebrows drew together, and he nodded to a mid-level mage.

The mage stepped forward. "It's bug magic."

I shuffled back, lowered myself to a clean spot on the ground, and waited for our fate to be decided.

The enforcers left us alone as they cleared the magic and took care of the three wolves who lived before they addressed us again.

I stared at the ground and listened to our surroundings until boots entered my field of vision. I craned my neck to see the elf enforcer. "Can I help you?"

"Give me your clothes. All of them." My wrist still hadn't healed, so I stumbled as I stripped and handed them over as I contemplated the many reasons the pockets sucked.

As soon as he stepped away, a healer came and patched up my gashes. His magic didn't work on me, so he made sure the bone in my arm would heal right and used bandages on the rest of my wounds. My arm would be good as new by morning, but it still throbbed like a bitch in heat as I slipped on the sack-like dress they gave me. At least Alex got healed. That was more important than my injuries.

The elf led us to the side as another team swept in. "I need your ID."

Elsie scanned hers first. I sighed in relief when it still showed her as an elite in the House of Umbra.

He held the portable scanner out and wiggled it. I begrudgingly scanned mine.

He frowned when he read it and handed it to another guy. "Verify this." His eyes swept over me. "We don't like when you people come to our pockets and cause trouble. Especially if you falsify documents." He pointed at Elsie. "You can go, but the hybrids stay until we sort this out."

Neither Alex nor I commented. I'd have words later with whoever changed my ID, though. It was much more believable when I was a stray Jonas adopted.

Elsie pointed toward the hotel. "I'll wait down the street."

I glanced that way and saw Glac leaning against a building. "Sure."

Alex put his hand on my arm so I didn't do something stupid. Like kick the elf in the groin and run. Tempting, but I wasn't *that* dumb.

I barely felt the familial stabbing in my chest before Gramps appeared. The Elf flinched.

I was fast, but Gramps was so quick that even vampire eyes couldn't see him coming. It gave me a new goal. I made a mental note to ask him how to reach it. "Princess Liliana is under the protection of Queen Ara of Umbra."

Alex snorted. "Princess Asshole is more like it."

I waved my good hand toward the crime scene. "As you can see by the dead wolves, we can protect ourselves."

The elf raised an eyebrow.

"Oh, yes. That attitude is quite helpful," Gramps drawled.

I shrugged. I didn't care how purebloods in Allure perceived my attitude.

Gramps managed to look both bored and perturbed at the same time.

Another goal. I was racking them up.

The elf ignored the exchange. "Thank you, Consort. Do you mind verifying her ID?"

Gramps appeared in front of the ID spell, and his head snapped my way. "Who changed this?"

"If I had to guess, I'd say Mathias."

His eyes narrowed. "Why?"

"Either to annoy me or because Jen told him to. Probably the former."

He turned his attention back to the elf. "You will keep this information to yourself until the formal announcement."

The elf bowed. "Of course."

His cold blue eyes focused on me. "And you will stop looking for fights."

"Wasn't looking," I said, fighting the urge to run to the gates and leave Allure behind. Based on the wolf attacks, the sense of doom, and the two idiots the dragons nabbed the day before, we weren't any safer there than in the human world.

Gramps leaned forward, the intensity in his eyes making the hairs on the back of my neck stand up. "Make a contract to stay out of trouble." It was an order.

I rolled my eyes. "Fine. I will stay out of trouble unless we're attacked, then I will fight like hell."

"Agreed." He disappeared before the contract snapped into place.

Elsie waited where I'd spotted Glac, who was gone. "You're not healing as fast as you should. You need blood."

I frowned. "I never need blood."

Her eyes focused on my still throbbing arm. "Your arm disagrees. As does your reaction time."

"My magic takes care of it."

"For now."

"I'm not like other vampires. Blood's not a requirement."

"I don't know much about natural-born vampires, but your healing is slower than the other day. Talk to your grandmother about it if you want, but you need blood."

I didn't go to the dragon bar that night. Instead, I rested and healed and thought about the mess that was my life. Dad always said that you had to break your problems down into pieces, deal with the ones you could, and let go of those you couldn't. I concluded everything was beyond my control except improving my magic. Cavil made a good point when he said I worried too much about hurting people when I used it. I needed to work on that.

As Alex and I headed to the renovated palace to check it out the next day, I decided to just roll with the family situation.

Elsie needed to take care of some personal business. She warned us to stay together like we were children or, worse, idiots. Alex watched her leave. "I really want to go home. It's not like we're any safer here than we were there."

"We're out of Mom and Dad's way here."

"I hate that."

I did, too.

I didn't expect to get into the castle as we joined the line of colorful paranormals waiting outside. And texting Jen or Mat would suck all the fun out of the adventure.

After a few minutes, Alex shifted his weight. "Why don't you just text them?"

"I want to see what happens."

"You want to cause trouble."

"That, too. Gotta keep Mat on his toes."

The Satyr in front of us turned and eyed me.

I gave her a pinky wave.

Alex's phone buzzed, and he took it out. "Mom says to behave ourselves. She means you. She wants me to keep you from causing more trouble."

"Fine. Come on, tattle-tale." I dragged him toward the front of the line. People protested as we pushed through the door.

A security station sat in front of a massive, warded wall with several guards checking people in and directing them to one of the two plush waiting areas where griffins organized tours. An oversized door behind the guard station led towards the back of the castle. It was closed.

"Well, this is disappointing. We can't see anything from here."

A guard raised his head and frowned. "State your business."

"Can you let Prince Mathias know Lily and Alex are here? Please."

"Do you have an appointment?"

"No. But he'll see us." I hoped. I planned to force him to give us a castle tour.

The guy messed with a magic device and pointed to the waiting area to his left. "You can wait there until the regent rejects your request. Then you must leave. On the off chance he agrees to see you, you will need to present your ID."

There was no place to sit in the waiting room, so we leaned against the back wall. I dropped into a trance to hear the surrounding conversations. The griffin guides organized tours of ten people, but none of them said anything worth eavesdropping on. After two groups were led away, I gave up and texted Mat.

> Did they tell you we're here to see you? Because we are. Surprise!

> A minute.

"I don't know what that means." I slid my phone into my jacket. "Does it mean wait a minute? He'll be out in a minute? Or do we have one minute to get lost?"

"It means he's not going to play your games."

"That sucks, because I really want to see what makes him tick."

A man named Pedro, or maybe Pablo, scanned our IDs. "This way, Princess." He didn't even try to keep the humor out of his voice.

It confirmed my suspicions that Mat changed my ID to mess with me. I'd need to say something like 'well played' to ensure he got the ego boost before I schemed a way to one-up him. My eyes were as big as saucers as we stepped through the doorway leading toward the back of the castle. "Wow. This is amazing."

The wood floors in the wide entryway gleamed. Two curved staircases swept up to the next floor on each side. The ceilings had to be four stories high. Arched doorways dotted the entry hall and led to opulent sitting areas.

We passed the stairs and through another arched doorway where an ancient male griffin waited. He nodded to our guide and then to us. "Princess Lily, Sir Alex, welcome to Castle Allure. I am George. This way."

We followed him through a modern kitchen the size of our entire house. White cupboards and light gray quartz countertops gleamed as the sunlight streamed through the bank of windows. More griffins rushed around preparing food using magic devices.

He ignored their greetings as he pointed to a breakfast nook. Even that was spacious and bright, with windows looking out on well-manicured courtyards, one with a swimming pool. A large, rectangular table took up the center of the room. Mat and Emine sat on one side, Jen and Drake on the other.

An ancient female griffin swept into the room. "Lily and Alex." She came over and took my hands. "Oh my. You're lovely." She patted Alex's arm. "And you are such a handsome young man. Sit. I'll get you some coffee and breakfast."

Jen jerked her thumb toward her. "That's Helen. She's the griffin matriarch."

I took the empty chair beside Drake. "This place is beautiful."

Alex slid into the one beside Emine and shot me a warning look. "Lily was going to take a tour without telling you."

"Alex is a tattletale." I rubbed my hands together. "So, Mat, what's up with the ID everyone says is fake? You messing with me?"

Humor danced in his eyes. "Everyone thinks it's fake, then?"

"Ahhh. I get it. The joke's on them *and* me." I leaned forward. "Gramps had to bail me out yesterday. I doubt he thinks it's funny."

Mat shrugged. "Emine runs the enforcers."

Jen looked back and forth between us. "Wait. What? I get constant lectures on my safety, and Lily gets funny games?"

Coffee landed in front of me. "Thank you, Helen." I turned my attention back to Jen. "You don't know how to defend yourself?"

"I'm not a warrior by any means, but I can hold my own. Especially now that I have functioning magic."

"Huh."

I almost flinched at the intensity of Mat's smile. "Lily is bored. She needs a challenge. I'm providing that. You are reckless and need to be reminded to think before you act. I also provide that. It's my duty as the eldest."

"I'm not bored."

"I'm not reckless."

"Lily is soooo bored. She needs to get out of here and back to her life," Alex said.

Emine leaned forward. "So you took out some tainted wolves yesterday? What was that about?"

"We were just walking down the street, and they jumped us. The elf enforcer didn't believe us because of my fake ID. Then Gramps, who followed us there, showed himself and confirmed my origins." I shot Mat the stink eye for good measure.

Drake cleared his throat. "Alex has a type of mental magic even my aunt hasn't seen before. There is no immunity to it, and he is a master at finding the thoughts he's interested in. Even my barriers wouldn't hold if he concentrated hard enough. Once he becomes better at his craft, no one will be safe. Especially since he can use his mental magic as a weapon. Even dragons can't do that, though we can usually confuse people and alter memories. The Bellicose want him for those abilities and because he can shift into a deadly predator. It makes him a valuable weapon."

"He's not interested in being a weapon. He wants to learn to shut it off so he can live his life." I took a bite of French toast.

"He wants you to stop answering for him," Alex mumbled.

"Does it work on vampires?" Jen asked.

"I've never met anyone who can block me, though you came close. With vampires, I have to work harder to read their thoughts. Lily and I are pretty sure our parents adopted us because we were too powerful for anyone else to handle."

"We don't doubt they love us. But yeah. That's probably why they took us in. I have to go to that stupid dinner at Ara's on Friday, and then we'll head out on Saturday. That attack proved we're not any safer here than we were at home. I suggest you compare notes with our parents."

Drake leaned around Jen. "Jonas and Ann Marie are working with me. I'm rooting out and eliminating the Bellicose."

"Then you're doing a shit job because they're setting up base camps all over the Treasure Valley. They were outside Dragon Headquarters when you were there, for fuck's sake." I realized everyone at the table went still. "What? It's true."

Jen cleared her throat. "Drake's doing a great job, but it's a little like playing whack-a-mole."

Alex pushed his plate away. "That's a good way to describe it. Lily's assessment is a little too harsh, but she's not wrong. From what I've seen, these guys only recruit lower-level paranormals. You guys treat low-powered people like humans treat poor people. After a while of being treated like crap, they build up resentment and anger. It only takes someone power-hungry enough to come along and harvest their anger, and you have a revolt."

"In this case, it's demons. I spotted one of their leaders recently."

Everyone's eyes turned to me. Mat leaned forward. "What did he look like?"

I blinked. "Dark hair and eyes, about six feet tall, lean muscle. He knew we were hiding in the shadows and smiled at us."

"The fake Jaques." Jen's voice shook.

Mat disappeared, reappeared before I could ask where he went, and shoved a picture in front of my face. "Is that the demon you saw?"

I examined the family portrait. My mother's cold, hard eyes stared at me with such contempt that I could almost hear her saying, 'Really, Liliana, it is beneath you to...' followed by almost everything I did. She didn't look much different other than the scar on the left side of her face and neck, which was absent.

I didn't recognize the man beside her. The consort, and allegedly one of my two fathers. The thought made me ill. I focused on the little kid version of Jen. She stood between the two adults with a tiny tiara on her head. Her eyes were so sad I had to look away. Mat and a man with dark hair and emotionless eyes stood on each side of the group like bookends.

I set the picture down. "Demons lie. They cheat, lie, and prey on any fear they can find." I tapped the picture. "They found yours. That is the man I saw, but it wasn't Jaques. A demon is using that form to prey on your fear."

She nodded. "I know. We already fought him once. His demeanor was all wrong."

"How do you know it's not him?" Emine asked.

"Because I can feel blood relations. That demon didn't register." When everyone continued to stare, I expanded. "Our mother used to go by a different name and wear glamor. She was pissed about Jaques's death. Something about him having the most potential. I think she was already pregnant with me when all that shit in Mahri went down." I shook my head to clear my thoughts. "She never referred to you two as her kids unless something triggered her. She was a cold, cruel bitch."

Emine put her hand on Mat's arm. "Just to be clear, what do you mean you feel family relations?"

I pointed to my chest. "I get tingling or stabbing in my chest when I come across blood relations. The closer the relation, the stronger the sensation. It's off the charts around Jed and these two. It's a little different with Ara and Quin, lighter somehow, and even lighter around Roman."

"Interesting." The tone of Mat's rough voice caused my spine to snap straight.

Alex cleared his throat. "Lily didn't want to meet you because her biological mother tried to make her a darker version of you, Jen. She thought she could use my sister to steal the ruling magic back. The woman convinced her you would either kill her on the spot or lock her up. Lily believed her after the way Jed treated her, so she avoided coming to Allure to let her magic out until it built up to dangerous levels. She's still convinced you're tricking her but is putting on a good front because she'd do anything to protect me. Our parents promised her they'd protect her from you until she made up her own mind. I don't sense she's there yet."

Unease caused me to clench my fists. "I would have preferred to go through my entire existence without meeting you. No offense. My point is the demon didn't register as family, so it's not Jaques."

Mat's eyes never left Alex. "Is that so?"

"I'm only telling you because the threat level in your voice makes me want to smash your brain." He held up a hand. "Which I will do if you come for Lily." The last came out in a growl.

"Nobody's smashing anyone's brains." Jen held up both hands. "And no one is going to hurt Lily. Geez, Mat. You think *I'm* the one that causes trouble?"

Drake dragged his eyes away from Alex. "You should heed that warning, Mathias. Alex and Lily are very protective of each other. He's only helping us because he thinks it's the right thing to do for his sister. In contrast, Lily sees helping us as sacrificing herself for her brother. Neither of them will hesitate to act to defend the other. They are Jonas's children, after all."

Emine grinned. "Whoo whee. This has taken an interesting turn. But then, it always does when Jen's involved. So, Lily, what happened with the wolves yesterday?"

"I gave my statement to the enforcers."

"That you did. But I want to know what really happened. Get me?"

I sighed. "Those wolves were outside your checkpoint yesterday. I even reported it to the castle guards, who gave me the fake ID. We walked when we left Meemaw's place because I had family overload. Something was off with that neighborhood, so I reported it to Glac. When they didn't find anything, we went to check it out. Stupid of me, I know. We killed a few of them. Also stupid, considering I'm a hybrid with a questionable ID. They transferred that nasty magic to us, even though we both took the immunity potion and we had to decontaminate. The enforcers released Elsie, but not us. Gramps vouched for us and swore the elf commander, or whatever he is, to secrecy."

"You're cool." Emine took a bite of toast. "I cleared you this morning."

"To get this conversation back on track, where was this demon you saw?" Jen asked.

"Roman says they're not there anymore, so it doesn't matter. I raided one of their offices and gave the info to my parents, so I'm sure you have it."

Drake stretched an arm across the back of Jen's chair. "Our latest information is that they want to kill Jen and Mat and take over the Coalition."

"That doesn't match what I know about demons." I tapped the table. "Demons feed on chaos and negative emotions. Specifically, human emotions. They don't care about paranormals or taking over anything. Their goal is only ever chaos."

Jen's eyebrows drew together. "We've already thought about that, but don't have answers. How do you know so much about demons?"

"I don't sleep much so I read a lot. That, mixed with the huge number of ancient books in Mom's library, means I've learned a lot of useless shit. My point is, look at how causing problems here helps them reach those goals."

"Lily's right," Alex said. "They already made sure a big chunk of people moved out of the pockets and into the human world. Including kids dumped by their parents with new powers they can't control. If it weren't for our parents, they would have already revealed themselves."

Jen held up a finger. "We're aware. And grateful. I'm learning how to create a pocket for you to retreat to."

Emine gave Jen a funny look as she stood. "I hate to break up this merry little reunion, but I have to get to work."

Mat stood with her. "I will walk you out." His eyes met mine. "I hope you know you are welcome here. You can use the family entrance in the back. I will reset the wards."

I watched them go. "What's up with the Jekyll-Hyde routine?"

Jen fake chuckled. "Besides the fact that you don't fit in one of his neat little boxes?"

"I don't fit in anywhere, so he might as well not try. Here's my theory. The demons learned most of the royal family died and had a window of opportunity to stir up trouble before you were old enough to rule. Then they figured out the second queen was desperate. So they team up with her to create chaos using the hybrids. It would have worked, but they didn't account for a First leading the outsiders. So, they had to step up their game."

"And what about the pockets?"

"Everyone knows the dragons and the lower-powered paranormals have been treated like crap by the Coalition for centuries, so they tried to use it to cause chaos amongst humans so they could feast. When that didn't work, they changed their plans. Demons are deceptive, but they're not short-sighted."

"They're trying to mind control them and inject them into the human world to create chaos?" Jen shook her head. "It's too easy. There's got to be more to it."

Drake sat up straight. "Perhaps. Perhaps not. They seem to think Alex is the key to whatever they are after."

"I can't get much from them because they're so singularly focused on their tasks." Alex rubbed his eyes. "I just want to live my life. Not fight demons."

"Same." I stood. "Well, I still have to get a dress for that stupid dinner. It's been real. It's been fun..."

Jen waved a hand. "Yeah, yeah. I'm going on a field trip today to absorb more mimic abilities. I can't wait to show you what I can do."

"Sure. Alex?"

Chapter Twenty

The rest of the week was quiet. Alex spent hours training with Deva, the Dragon Queen. He made huge strides in developing and learning to control his mental magic, and I was proud of him.

But I didn't do well in zero drama climates, so I struggled to mind my manners. Don't get me wrong, I had a great time with the dragons at the bar and even visited Jen and Meemaw. But I was still bored, homesick, off my game, and running on emotional overload. I wanted to go home and find a new toxic workplace.

Which is why I hesitated outside the entrance to the vampire castle on Friday night. I was decked out in a seafoam green cocktail dress that the fairy at the dress shop insisted I wear. It was backless with a halter front and flowed from my hips, hitting just below my knees. The matching shoes were spelled for comfort. I liked them so much that I bought a pair of boots that would allow my claws to extend and retract without damaging them.

I stood outside the gates and tried not to fidget as my stomach soured at the prospect of seeing Jed. Every time I'd left the dragon district, and a few times while inside it, I felt his people watching. But Ara told me not to give him any information with a gleam in her eye that said she was hunting. No way I'd get between her and her prey. So, I stood outside the gates and pretended my stomach wasn't trying to revolt.

Jed appeared in the flashing circle with four of his vampires. The mage who used his flashing abilities as a taxi service inclined his head and disappeared. Several mages made a decent living in Allure flashing people around. I envied them. When I used my flashing abilities, I maimed everyone I passed.

Jed wore a tuxedo that accentuated his dark good looks, but did nothing to hide his slimy demeanor. He stopped in front of me and bared his teeth in a fake smile. "Liliana. Thank you for coming and for dressing appropriately."

"I'm not here for you, Jed." I hit the timer on my watch. Ara convinced me to come for two hours and I wasn't staying a second longer than I had to.

His fake smile turned feral as he offered me his arm. "Very well. Let's go in, shall we?"

I ignored his arm and marched toward the gate. "Sure. Let's get this over with."

"Now, Liliana. We need to be on our best behavior tonight. I know it's difficult for a mongrel like you, but you must at least try to impress my mother."

"Mongrel, eh? I thought I was an abomination. You need to make up your mind, Jed."

He didn't comment as we strode through the gate and down the walkway surrounded by his vampires. Elsie hung back, blending in with the other elites.

A vampire in a tuxedo led us to a sitting room where a few people sat sipping pink champagne. Another appeared in front of us with a tray. My hand didn't shake as I took a glass, so I considered it a win. A woman with long, dark hair and a revealing red gown approached. "Hello, Jedediah. I see you brought one of your whores to entertain us."

"Rudeness must run in the family," I mumbled.

Jed shot me a warning look. "Vesna. I wish it were a pleasure to see you. This is Liliana, my daughter."

I didn't bother to correct the name because it was fitting for a man that I despised calling me a name I also hated. I took another gulp of champagne.

Vesna's eyes scanned me before she threw her head back and laughed. "How did you figure out how to turn a mage, brother? It's almost worth traveling here to see Mother's reaction to this mistake."

I loved me some drama, even when it centered on yours truly. But I wasn't in the mood, so I examined the other guests. Roman and his pal

Folami were across the room with Ara. Quin was tucked into the shadows, where he could hear every conversation. Another skill I needed to learn.

Jed leaned toward his sister. "You don't understand the slightest thing about hybrids."

I almost spit out my drink. Talk about the ignorant preaching to the oblivious. "So, Jed, you know a lot about hybrids?"

He gripped my arm a little too hard. "I know a great deal more than my sister, yes."

I grabbed a fresh drink off a passing tray. Then almost dropped it when Quin appeared next to Vesna. His eyes flipped from me to Jed. "Release her arm before I break yours."

It was going to be a long two hours.

A cruel smile spread across Vesna's face. "Yes, Jedediah, release your recent mistake. Creating a mage-vampire hybrid will not win you the title of heir."

Jed ignored her. "Father, this is Liliana, the woman you insisted I present. You'll find I have met Mother's deadline."

Quin's eyes scanned me. "Yes. A family dinner is the appropriate place for an introduction."

I fought not to smile at his sarcasm.

"Dinner will be served shortly, so we shall move to the dining room," Ara announced.

I wasted no time following Quin as he zipped in that direction. The places were all set with name cards on them. Mine was at the foot of the table, leaving three chairs between me and the other guests. "That's not awkward at all," I mumbled as a drive-by vampire held my chair out.

Jed stopped behind his chair and motioned toward me. "What is this about, Mother?"

Ara's eyes sparkled in a way that made me wonder if family drama was her version of the toxic workplace. I could respect that. "I'm good down here."

"Please sit, Jedediah. We are here to celebrate Roman's reemergence, not worry about semantics."

Roman and Folami moved their place settings to either side of me rather than sitting with the family. I appreciated the gesture.

Jed lowered himself into his assigned seat beside Gramps. "You would choose that...my daughter over your real family?"

Roman aligned his silverware before answering. "Oh, yes, Jedediah. Lily lives in my territory, you see, and we've become close allies. In fact, I'd like to think we share a mentor-student relationship. Besides the many advantages she brings to my territory, including allowing me to acquire some high-powered vampires who encroached, she is much more vibrant and interesting than you. I very much like her company and plan to preserve our alliance for many years. I do not see a problem with that, but if you do, I'd love to hear it."

A chill ran down my spine when his magic ramped up. It wasn't until that moment that I realized Roman's long-winded speeches were cover for something much more dangerous. I knew he was super old, but he'd always been nice to me and even tried to teach me. So, when Jed's eyes lowered and Vesna flinched, I understood I'd been playing with fire in my flippant ignorance. I made a mental note to be more observant in the future.

"That is very kind of you to take an active interest in Lily." Ara raised her glass toward Roman.

As she steered the conversation away from me, I checked my watch and gulped down another drink.

The rest of the dinner went well. I kept my head down and focused on my food while the group made small talk about recent politics and the unrest in the pockets. Based on their discussion, one thing was for sure. Jen needed to get up to speed on her magic and gain self-confidence fast if she hoped to keep her throne.

I still had fifteen minutes left when we finished dessert. My feet danced under the table with the need to get the hell out of there.

Ara waited until a drive-by vampire served coffee before waving her hand. A rush of magic swept through the room. It floated over me in a soft caress. Flyby vampires zipped around, and the doors slammed closed.

I jumped. Or I would have if I could move. She'd somehow trapped us all in our own skin. I poked at the sensation. It felt an awful lot like my magic right before it turned violent. I stabbed at it again. My ears popped when it released me. "Oops." I squirmed in my chair.

Her feral smile caused the hair on the back of my neck to stand up and make me glad I was on her good side. "Good job, Lily. Now, let's get down to business, shall we?"

"Yes, my love." Quin patted her hand. Apparently, her command to freeze didn't work on him, either. "Tell us about the hybrid, Jedediah."

Jed unfroze and set his coffee down. He tried to appear calm, but the tremor in his hand gave him away. "What would you like to know?"

Quin rested his elbows on the table and steepled his fingers. "Her origins."

Jed wiped his forehead with his napkin. "Of course. She is the result of an accident. I had to turn her as an infant to save her life."

Ara leaned forward. "Is that so?"

"Yes, Mother. She was a mistake I tried to rectify, nothing more. When she developed her vampire powers early, her mother transferred her to my house because she could not control her. Feral little thing she was. My blood bond did not work, so I had to go to great lengths to contain her. I planned to transfer the mistake to your house for elimination. She's rather addled, you see." Jed's head hung in fake remorse. "The sorceress Ann Marie destroyed my property and ran away with the girl so she could raise a weapon. The abomination has recently manipulated Roman into stealing several of my top vampires and killed others."

I couldn't stop my snort. I spent a lot of years in therapy dealing with the abuse I suffered in the months I spent under Jed's care. The spin he put on it didn't surprise me, but his bullshit was as colorful as it was selfish.

Ara ignored me. "Is that so?"

"The hybrid can be part of my house. I'm sure I am strong enough to blood bond her if you want to sweep Jedediah's mess under the rug, Mother. I'm in desperate need of a new maid," Vesna said.

"Of course you are, dear." Ara released her hold on the table without lifting a finger. Neat.

Jed took a sip of coffee. He oozed confidence and arrogance. "That is the truth of what happened. As you know, Ann Marie is formidable. I could not retrieve my mistake from her."

"How?" Quin asked.

Jed's eyes flashed red. "Pardon?"

"How did you turn an infant?"

"It is quite a long story involving her irresponsible mother."

Ara's expression melted into sorrow. "Anitta was not irresponsible, nor did she make those kinds of mistakes."

I shivered at my mother's name. "I agree. She knew what she was doing."

"Exactly." Ara's pained sigh broke my heart. "I tried to give you the benefit of the doubt. It's disappointing that you would scheme against me and lie to my face. I cannot let that go unpunished."

Jed's arrogance didn't melt like I'd expected. "You accuse me of lying?"

Quin slid a piece of paper in front of Jed. "How did those vampires die?"

Jed examined the list. "The hybrid is prone to temper tantrums. Members of my house paid the price."

Everyone's attention turned to me. My heart jumped into my throat. The asshole was trying to pin his abuse on me to get out of trouble. By their dead, blank stares, I wasn't sure my initial fear of being tortured by my biological family wasn't valid. I clasped my hands on my lap and squared my shoulders, but didn't comment.

Quin smiled. I think. It was hard to tell with him. "How many vampires did you kill when you left Jedediah's house?"

"Three, possibly four." My voice sounded much more confident than I felt.

"Did you return to house Jedediah to get revenge?"

"No. And my mom had nothing to do with the escape. I blew up the place, ran away, and never looked back. A lone wolf took me in that night and contacted my parents. I've been with them ever since."

"I assure you, Lily is not feral. She doesn't even hunt." Roman came to my rescue. "I do not recommend trying to force her into servitude, however. Jonas and Ann Marie First raised her to be independent and lethal. Her vampire skills are those of a turned vampire ten times her age. I still have not assessed them all."

Vesna shook her head. "You have been dormant for a long time, uncle. Perhaps your judgment is skewed. No matter the age when turned, young vampires still take years to develop enough power to function without guidance. The hybrid's blood is weak. It will take her much longer."

I knew that was true of other vampires, but those rules never applied to me. I could tolerate the sun and didn't need blood. On top of that, I was super fast for my age. I'd always credited my mage side, but maybe it came from being a natural-born vampire.

"Oh, yes. I'm sure Roman's dormancy is the reason for his opinion." Quin didn't take his eyes off me as he handed the list of names to Ara. "All but four vampires perished after Jonas First took in the hybrid."

Ara glanced at the list that she didn't need to read, considering she felt every vampire death and remembered most of them. "As a mother, I have always tried to give my children the benefit of the doubt." She folded her hands. "Lilith once held the philosophy that the firstborn should lead the vampires. She even named Roman as her heir. He did not have the power or the will to hold the position. The more she tried to force the issue, the more ruling magic I gained. Magic highly favors the number three, you see. And no one can change that, no matter how powerful." She took Quin's hand. "She almost killed my match and killed our sister. The sacrifice helped her take away my ability to have an heir."

The room was silent, and Roman's head bowed.

Ara leaned forward, the sadness melting into rage. "Because of her actions, magic gifted me with nearly as much power as Lilith. She was livid, so she ensured her ruling magic would skip me and transfer to the heir I'd never have. Then she chose permanent sleep."

The table was silent. Everyone's heads bowed except for mine. I kept my guard up and my attention on Quin. I figured if anyone were going to attack me, it would be him.

My eyes flipped to Ara when she shifted in her seat. When she had my attention, she continued. "This caused Jedediah and Vesna to assume I could and would make one of them my heir. Their competitions have kept us entertained and harmed very few, so I allowed it to continue. I am sorry, granddaughter, that my inaction has caused you such pain and suffering."

My stomach flipped as I blinked back tears that tried to fall. What an awful existence that must have been. "I'm sorry that happened to you, Meemaw. And that you never got your heir."

"Meemaw?" Jed stood and pointed at me. "That is not your grandchild. She is a mistake and an abomination!"

Ara was out of her chair and across the table before I could blink. She used one arm to raise him off the floor and pinned him against the wall. Claws formed in one hand and tore out his vocal cords. Then she stabbed him in the stomach several times before leaning in and whispering something I didn't catch.

My heart thudded so hard I was sure the entire table heard it, but I didn't dare move a muscle. My meemaw was a badass. But as much as I always wanted to see Jed bleed, her speed and precision were as terrifying as they were impressive.

Jed fell to the floor, limp.

I tore my eyes away from the carnage when Meemaw turned her attention to me. Every hair on my body raised. She retracted her claws and wiped her bloody hands on her dress. "Thank you, dear. You are a true gem."

"Umm…"

She waved a hand. Everyone in the room except Quin flinched. "As I was saying, I have been very lenient with my children. I wanted to give them the benefit of the doubt. The power that comes with royalty and the belief that one of them would become my heir has gone to their heads. It is a mistake I plan to rectify."

I nodded my shaky head because I didn't know what else to do. Ara's calm, conversational demeanor while torturing her own son wasn't something I could process in a matter of seconds. Don't get me wrong, I had no sympathy for Jed. But I didn't know where the conversation was going, and was certain it would be awful for me. Hopefully, I wouldn't end up in a pool of my own blood in the corner of the dining room.

"My children have made the mistake of thinking my leniency gives them the right to lie to me. They assume because I have not mentioned their lies, I believe them. What is your opinion about that, Lily?"

I clasped my hands so hard my knuckles turned white. "Lying is a waste of time because people almost always uncover the truth. My dad says that only people willing to deceive themselves can present lies well to others."

She pointed at me, and I fought not to flinch. "Exactly right. My children have forgotten that." Ara tapped her chin. "Now, Vesna. Tell me about the vampire named Scott."

Vesna swallowed. "He was a vampire transfer who ran away. I tried to catch him, but I fear he's gone feral."

"From where?" Quin asked.

"From Jedediah's house. I took pity on him and took him in a few years ago."

"And when you tried to use him as a bargaining chip, he ran from you," Ara concluded. "You kept him because he knew about Lily."

"I didn't know about the hybrid." Vesna's voice was two octaves higher, and the pungent scent of her fear mixed with the salty odor of Jed's blood made it hard to keep my fangs from popping out. I'd worked hard to control my fangs so I could present myself as a human, but the adrenaline rush made it more difficult.

"And you never asked him why he left Jedediah's house?" Meemaw asked.

"The vampire would not talk about his reasons no matter how...persuasive I tried to be."

It was a whopper of a lie, and we all knew it. Vesna totally knew about me.

Ara hung her head. "Lily, please tell me about the vampire Scott."

I tried to place the name. "Scott?"

"He was a perimeter guard during your time with Jedediah."

I'd blocked a lot of that out, so I had to dig deep. "Is he blonde? A somewhat new vampire?"

"Correct."

"I don't remember much about him, only that he and a few other guards were nice to me. They brought me clothes and food and tried to teach me when they could."

Quin turned his attention to Vesna. "Scott is now a member of our house. You knew about Lily and hid the knowledge from your mother."

Vesna flipped her hair over her shoulder. "It is true I heard about her, Father. But I did not know she was real."

Ara responded by pinning her like she did Jed. It happened so fast that I jumped. Roman, who stayed in a vampire trance throughout the conversation, latched onto my arm with a little too much strength.

When she finished gutting her own daughter, Ara straightened her bloody dress and turned her attention back to me. "I apologize for the actions of my children. Your friend Scott is a wonderful addition to my house. We share a love of cooking."

"That's...good." I crossed my ankles to keep from acting on the sudden urge to run away. I needed to finish my two hours and get the hell out of Dodge.

Ara's smile sent another shiver down my spine. "Quite." Her smile melted away, and her eyes filled with sorrow. "I did not want dinner to go like this."

I hated seeing the pain in her eyes. No mother wanted to learn their kids were liars and cheats. "Sorry, Meemaw. I can't imagine how hard this is for you."

"Oh, my. You are a delight." She folded her hands in front of her and ignored the blood pooling around her feet. "I never had the opportunity to have a third child. I know you do not want to hear this, but as you said, it is best to be honest." She closed her eyes as if gathering her thoughts, and I dreaded her next words. "You are the third born of my line and have inherited the power of Lilith. Therefore, you are my rightful heir."

Tingling started at my hairline and spread. I recognized the feeling. It was the same feeling I had when Dad hunted me in his spinosaurus form. It meant I was either about to lose the fight or in serious trouble. I tried to yank my arm out of Roman's grip so I could run, but he wouldn't let go. I shook my head so hard my neck pinched. "Nope. I have a life."

She sighed. "I am aware. Unfortunately, magic has chosen you, and there is nothing either of us can do about it. But don't worry. You have plenty of time to let it sink in because I don't plan to go to sleep or die for a few millennia. Lilith's power is why Jedediah could not force a blood bond on you and why you are not feral. Not even I could force you into the fold so you can have some of the same freedom you always enjoyed."

Beep. Beep. Beep.

My two hours were up. I slammed my hand onto my watch and stared at it, gobsmacked. Stupefied. Shocked. For some strange reason, my brain turned to the night I met Cavil. He tried to tell me I wasn't a vampire or a mage. Even the origin mages said I had the magic of Lilith. But I held on to my delusions that it didn't matter. That my mixed heritage disqualified me from... whatever this was. I craned my neck to look at Jed, then bent over and lost my dinner on the rug.

Flyby vampires filled the room. One shoved some kind of concoction into my hand while another cleaned up my mess. I slammed the drink, heaved again, and put a napkin over my mouth. "Is there a restroom I can use?"

Ara was around the table before I finished the sentence and linked her arm with mine. She patted my hand, leaving a smear of blood on it. "Of course. This way, dear."

I closed the door of the powder room and tried to heave again, but couldn't because of the damn concoction they gave me. As I splashed cold water on my face, I remembered I wore makeup and raised my head to look in the mirror. Smudged mascara made me look like a zombie. The thought that being a zombie would have been easier to deal with than being an heir floated through my mind. Dismissing the thought, I used the hand soap to wash it off, then rinsed my mouth. "This can't be happening." After a few deep breaths, I decided it was time to face the music and swung the bathroom door open.

Ara stood outside, her arms crossed across her bloody chest. "I have no plans to harm my heir."

"Okay." I shuffled from one foot to the other. "So, what does this mean?"

"We shall see. There's no reason for anything in your life to change right now, though I do hope to get to know you better. I only wanted you to know the truth. Come, dear. I will walk you out."

"Sure." I followed her on shaky legs as she led me to the mansion's door.

Quin fell in behind, and I wondered if it was to contain me if I freaked out and attacked Ara. Elsie met us outside.

Ara kissed my cheek. "I know this is quite a shock, and I apologize for that. Please don't let this revelation drive you away. I do so look forward to getting to know you. Not as an heir, but as my granddaughter."

"What's going to happen to Jed?" I didn't care what happened to him or his sister, but it was the only sane thing I could think to say.

"I plan to punish my children like any other House Master who steps out of line. For now, they will remain where they are as a warning to others." She patted my cheek. "If you wish to put them in one of your beautiful boxes, I am fine with that."

I blinked at the glee in her voice. "Um. I don't know if that's a good idea."

Her tinkling laugh echoed through the night. "Of course, dear. Please come by in the morning before you leave."

"Sure." My feet edged toward the gate.

Ara grinned. "Good." She kissed my cheek again.

I turned to Quin, who stood two inches in front of a guard's face, staring at him. "Night, Gramps."

He inclined his head and melted into the night.

I high-tailed it out of there. Elsie and I were halfway down the street before I spoke. "Did you know?"

"Everyone knew except you. You radiate magic like a fireplace radiates heat."

"So Jed knew."

"Probably. Roman and his partner, too."

"Why didn't they tell me?"

"Because they couldn't until the queen acknowledged you as her heir. It's forbidden."

I got lost in my tangled thoughts as we continued to walk at a human pace. When we rounded the corner near the gates to the neighborhood, I stopped.

CHAPTER TWENTY-ONE

PALACE GUARDS AND GRIFFINS lined the castle's wall, gargoyles inter-mingled between them. As one, they turned in our direction.

"Oh, hell no." I couldn't deal with any more shit that night, so I went fluid and out the gate.

Elsie caught up with me halfway down the block.

A tingle between my shoulder blades continued until we turned the corner away from the upscale neighborhood. "Do you feel that?"

Elsie gave me an odd look, then wrapped the shadows around us as she scanned the surrounding area. "I don't feel anything."

I focused on my senses. "Nothing now." With one last glance back, I continued down the street. The events of the night addled my brain. "Let's get out of here."

We went fluid until we came to the creepy neighborhood where the wolves attacked. Elsie latched onto my arm to stop me. "I feel it now."

"Yeah." I wrapped shadows around us.

Elsie followed suit, only she did it better. Power of Lilith, my ass. "Who taught you about shadows?"

"No one." I scanned the street as the feeling grew stronger, then tilted my head to see the top of the buildings. "We need to get out of here."

"Fast," she added.

We went fluid and zipped through the neighborhood and stopped at the edge.

I slunk to the side of the building and shook out my hands. "Do you feel it?"

"Yes."

"What do you suppose it is?"

"Nothing good."

I pulled out my phone. "What is this district called?"

"The mixed district. We're next to the maginet infrastructure building."

I texted the information to Mat. When he confirmed he was on the way, I slid my phone into the pocket of my dress and hoped it didn't fall out if I had to fight.

The feeling of unease grew. "Demons?"

"Maybe. Though they don't usually feel this potent."

"Great." It was a shitty end to a shitty day.

A familial stab zinged through my chest a second before Mat appeared in the middle of the street.

Elsie zipped out, grabbed him, and wrapped the shadows around the three of us.

I wiped my sweaty palms on my blood-streaked dress. "Do you feel it?"

"Yes." His golden eyes scanned the area. "Leave and get to safety."

I shook my head. "Did you know our dad used to surprise attack us in the middle of the night?"

Mat's eyebrows drew together. "I don't see what that has to do with the current situation."

"He believed we should be prepared to fight at any time of the day or night. He'd train us at every opportunity. Offering nuggets of wisdom, showing us how to adult, or a new way to problem-solve. He and Mom made sure we were prepared for anything life threw at us." I met Mat's eyes. "Ever been chased through the woods by a Spinosaurus while dodging magical tripwires set by a sorceress as a mental mage attacks you?"

"Your point?"

"I can take care of myself." I pointed down the street. "Whatever's out there is after my brother and wants me dead. It's going to take more than you to eliminate it, and I'll be damned if I hide while other people fight my battles."

Mat scanned my face, then inclined his head. "Noted."

The three of us stood shoulder-to-shoulder in silence and scanned the street.

Click. Click. Click.

A creature slithered out of the darkness.

Mat held up his hand in a wait gesture.

Click. Click. Click.

The thing swung its long, triangular head toward a nearby building and tilted it up. It scrunched its body and lowered its front legs like a cat ready to pounce. Except cats didn't have bodies that looked like an accordion. Nor were they ten feet long.

"I can box it in." My voice was so quiet only Mat and Elsie could hear.

"Not yet."

A different familial stab reverberated through my chest. "Gramps is nearby."

Mat's hard eyes turned to me. "Gramps?"

I shrugged. "Quin. He hates the name."

His lip twitched, but he didn't comment.

The creature froze in its pounce position.

I felt Gramps stop on the other side of the street.

Click. Click. Click.

Another creature appeared. Then more. And more. There had to be at least ten of them.

We didn't move. Didn't even breathe.

"Don't box them until they attack," Mat said.

The first creature thrust its head forward.

A stream of black goo whizzed past us.

I sent my magic toward two of them and willed it to create a box. I added the intention of destroying and banishing. When I flipped on my magic sight, it took away my night vision. I blinked to adjust. A blood-red solid box formed around the two demons.

One clawed at the sides, trying to escape. Razor-sharp blender things formed inside and whirled without making a sound. The two demons exploded into a chunky mass of greenish-yellow slime and melted to ash. I released the box. "Gross."

Mat conjured two glowing blue short swords. "Your magic is effective."

"No shit."

A mass of triangular heads swung toward us.

Mat's eyes took on a golden glow. "Charge!"

Dragons appeared out of nowhere, including Drake.

Gramps emerged under one creature, a sword in his hand, his claws and fangs out.

Elsie fell in behind me as I went fluid and flung magic at a creature who spit goo at my drinking buddy, Flintous. I wouldn't have known it was him if he hadn't taken me for a drunken ride a couple of nights before. Deva spotted us and put a stop to it before we made it to the top of the hotel. It was still fun. During our little excursion, I noticed a long scar on his side just under his wing, which made him easy to identify.

The box I created wasn't as well-formed as the first one, but it worked.

Flintous's enormous head swung in my direction and lowered in what I interpreted as a nod.

I didn't have time to respond because a creature pounced toward me. I dropped to the ground, rolled, and stabbed my claws into its underbelly and ripped. Green goo poured over my fancy new dress. I blasted the wounds with a knockout spell intending to banish it, then went fluid toward where I sensed Mat.

The green goo creature exploded, showering the entire area in dust.

A stream of dragon fire shot in front of my face and blinded me.

An arm snaked around my waist, and I crashed to the bloody ground.

"Stay down!" Mat's voice almost blew out my ear.

"Boom!"

He let go of me and hopped to his feet. Blind and deaf, I blinked and rubbed my sensitive ears. They were ringing so loud it made me dizzy. I shook my head and punched out at a figure in front of me.

"It's me."

My senses came back online. "Holy shit."

Mat smiled. It was so intense that I wasn't sure if I should run or smile back. "Emine has arrived."

I turned back to the fight. Gramps gutted a creature, then cut off its head in the blink of an eye.

I dodged a crater in the center of the cobblestone street and attacked one of the three remaining demons as it scrambled to escape the intense light created by whatever Emine did. "She's...effective."

"She likes to blow shit up," a woman's voice came from behind us.

I spun toward Emine, retracted my claws, and went in for a fist bump. Emine obliged, then waved a hand toward me. "You dress up for the occasion?"

"Something like that. Three left." I boxed one but couldn't get the other two because Elsie and Gramps were in the way, so I went fluid to help Elsie.

She had her claws lodged into two diamond-shaped slits that resembled eyes. I slammed my claws into its neck and sent magic through them.

Elsie landed in a crouch when it turned to dust.

I spun toward the last one, but it was gone. I marched toward Mat. "How in the hell are demons in Allure without Jen knowing?"

Mat's eyebrows drew together. "What do you mean?"

My eyes flipped to Gramps for help, but he was busy polishing his sword.

I jammed a finger in the direction of the castle. "Do any of you pure-bloods read? Those gargoyles can sense demons. Which means they know where, how many, and what type they are. Jen is their queen. Why isn't she using them?"

Mat's face hardened. "She is an ineffective queen."

I threw my hands in the air. "Bullshit. She's new and needs confidence, but she's done a lot in the last couple of years. Even my parents are impressed."

His eyebrows drew together, and he shook his head as if to clear it.

"Right. Never mind. Not my problem. I'm out of here in the morning, anyway. Come on, Elsie. Thanks for the assist, Gramps. See you around, Emine." I went fluid and headed toward the hotel. I needed a shower and a drink.

The morning sun crested over the horizon, warming the ground and evaporating the dew as I made my way to Cavil's house. I wanted to let him know we were leaving, so I headed out while Elsie and Alex finished getting ready. They agreed to meet me at my grandparents' place in an hour.

A couple of humongous shifters with flat noses guarded the gates. The biggest one examined me from head to toe. "State your business."

"I need to see Cavil for a minute."

"No appointment, no entry."

I sighed. "I'll text him."

Cavil's witch stepped out the door, her heels clicking on the walkway. "The God Cavil no longer wishes to associate with you."

The head shifter turned toward her and folded his arms.

"Oh?" After I sent my text, I held up my phone. "I guess we'll see."

Cavil stormed out the door, his sunny disposition gone as he eyed the witch. "Your services are no longer needed."

Her fists clenched. "But she's only a hybrid."

"You're wrong." He slapped a hand on her and disappeared, then reappeared in front of me.

I almost didn't jump. "Hey, Cavil. We're heading home this morning. I wanted to say goodbye." I eyed the shifters. "Already building your cult, eh?"

His face lit up. "I have gained some faithful followers. The queen herself put these shifters in my care. They are honorable and a solid addition."

"Yes. Even a mongrel like me can see that."

The smile melted off his face. "It won't happen again. Treating hybrids with respect is in the employment contracts."

"Unnecessary, but thank you. So, you're going to live here from now on?"

"No. I'll relocate to the farmhouse after it's renovated."

Butterflies erupted in my stomach. "Okay."

His sunshine smile eclipsed my dark mood. "It will be full of the things I like."

Elsie and Alex appeared down the street and made their way to me at a human pace. "That's great. I'm happy for you." I took a second to appreciate his gorgeousness. The butterflies disappeared as I realized he was way out of my league, so there was no point in letting him affect me. "Well. I just thought I'd let you know we're leaving. Have fun with your cronies."

Cavil's eyes reflected concern. "See you in a few days, Lily."

The exchange was all sorts of awkward. I didn't look back as I met Alex and Elsie. "What are you doing here? I thought we were going to meet at Ara's."

Alex shot me a dirty look and took off down the street to talk to a guard who waited for us near the intersection.

"Mistress Ara wouldn't like me leaving you alone. Especially after last night," Elsie said.

"We don't even know if those creatures were after me."

"Doesn't matter. It's my duty to fight next to you."

I sighed. "Are you sure you want to stay with me, Elsie? The human world has a lot more laws and rules, and I don't want a house."

"You'll make an excellent master."

"When you go feral from the lack of supervision, don't say I didn't warn you."

"That won't happen. Besides, being the second in command to the heir is an honor no vampire would pass up. Even if it means importing blood to stay hidden from humans."

Bile rose to my throat at the thought of running a vampire house. "Nope. I don't have, nor do I plan to have a house."

"It doesn't matter how big your house is. Even if I'm your only vampire, it's an honor. And I'll make an excellent second."

My stomach eased. Elsie was too serious for my taste, but I doubted I could get out of taking her with me. Nor did I have the energy or emotional capacity to fight about it. "Whatever."

She grinned. "Don't worry. I have things to wrap up here before I move in with you. It could take a couple of weeks."

"Sure." Maybe she'd change her mind.

Meemaw stood at the door and gave me one of her surprise hugs. "I know you are eager to leave, dear, but I do hope you come back soon."

I tried to give her a sincere smile, but all I could think about was the nonchalant way she gutted her kids. "Okay. My offer to come visit still stands." I hoped she didn't take me up on it for a while.

She clutched her hands to her chest. "I cannot wait."

We hightailed it out of there.

"I'll be glad to get home, where I understand our security and strategy." Alex threw his bag in the back of my van.

"What happened to our groceries?"

He shook his head. "Mom came and got them. I thought I told you that."

"Nope." I threw my bag in and headed toward the passenger side. "You're driving. I need time to think about my situation. Elsie declared herself my second in command. I guess she's coming to live with us."

"No kidding?" Alex slid a pair of sunglasses on. "It'll be good to have someone who doesn't sleep much to monitor the security."

True.

We made good time back toward the valley. The drive from our house to Allure usually took about an hour and a half. We were on paved roads in less than an hour. "I can't wait to get home."

Alex grinned. "Me too. I don't know why Mom sent us there. It wasn't like we were any safer."

"The dragons made us much safer than the wards around our house. It was only when we left their territory that things went sideways."

"If you say so. Those infected guys drifted through all the time, and the dragons didn't notice until I pointed them out."

"Yeah. They're not even using the gargoyles to find demons. I hope Jen fixes that problem soon." I leaned my head back and closed my eyes.

Boom!

My heart pounded in my ears as my eyes flew open.

A sharp pain exploded through my head. My neck snapped back and forth. The seatbelt cut into my chest. I realized the van was rolling.

Someone screamed.

When the roof above me collapsed, I ducked down and tried to hold on as spots danced in front of my eyes. There was a steep slope on my side, and we were rolling down it. I turned my head to look at Alex, but couldn't focus.

The movement came to an abrupt stop.

My head banged against the door with a 'thud.' Spots rolled over my vision as the stench of gasoline, earth, and blood clogged my nose. Thankful to still be conscious, I grasped for the seatbelt release.

A massive fist flashed in the corner of my vision. Everything went black.

My eyes wouldn't open, and everything ached. My head pounded. I tried to move an arm. Nope.

I felt myself being lifted and the wind brushing against my skin. What happened? It felt like someone replaced my brain with cotton. My thoughts swam as I fought to stay conscious. Whoever carried me jostled. The pain was so intense I couldn't hold on. I slipped back into the darkness.

When my eyes opened again, I was in my own bed. The stabbing pain running through my chest told me Jen and Gramps were in the room. "What the fuck are you doing here?"

"You almost died, and that's the first question you ask?" Jen's voice held a touch of amusement.

"Yeah." I tried to sit up, but my head swam, so I collapsed. I refocused my energy on trying to remember what happened. It all came rushing back. Heading home. Alex driving. Something hit us, and we rolled.

"Drink this."

Gramps shoved something into my hand, and I cracked an eye open. "I don't need blood."

Jen shook her head. "I healed you, but without blood, you're going to stay lethargic."

I shoved the blood bag toward her. "I'll be fine."

Gramps leaned over me, his blue eyes dull. "Oh, yes. I am sure you know much more about vampire physiology than me."

I frowned and tried to remember why it was important to heal. My head was too fuzzy. "I can't think."

"Because you need blood. Drink." It was an order.

I plugged my nose and chugged the blood, then closed my eyes. Gramps was right. I could almost feel my cells knitting themselves back together and my energy levels rising. Alex was going to laugh at that. I launched myself into a sitting position. *"Where's Alex?"*

Jen's face softened. "I'm sorry, Lily."

"No." Tears spilled out of my eyes. I raised a trembling hand and swiped them away. I swallowed, unsure if I wanted to ask the next question. "Tell me."

"Quin said he was alive when they took him." She held up a hand. "Glacintial is following them and will bring him back."

My world dropped out from under me.

Please take a moment to leave a review on Amazon.

Crowns and Curses, Book 3, is scheduled for release in December. It takes the fight to the human world, deals with the fallout from Anitta's attempted coup, and is full of a bunch of mystery and mayhem.

Sign up for my newsletter at www.mlconklin.com to stay updated on upcoming releases.

Thank you to everyone who helped me with this book. The editors, proofreaders, beta readers, and ARC readers were all amazing to work with and continue to make me a better writer, one criticism at a time. The cover designers at getcovers.com did a great job bringing the world to the front with little information.

A special shoutout to my furry assistants, Callie and Gracie, for sitting in front of the screen judging me while I try to write, and Zorro for all his k-9 cuteness.

And thank you for reading this series. You are the best.

Cheers.

ML Conklin